12⁵⁰

D0786791

A FISTFUL
OF EMPTY

A FISTFUL OF EMPTY

BENJAMIN M. SCHUTZ

VIKING

VIKING
Published by the Penguin Group
Viking Penguin, a division of Penguin Books USA Inc.,
375 Hudson Street, New York, New York 10014, U.S.A.
Penguin Books Ltd, 27 Wrights Lane,
London W8 5TZ, England
Penguin Books Australia Ltd, Ringwood,
Victoria, Australia
Penguin Books Canada Ltd, 2801 John Street,
Markham, Ontario, Canada L3R 1B4
Penguin Books (N.Z.) Ltd, 182–190 Wairau Road,
Auckland 10, New Zealand

Penguin Books Ltd, Registered Offices:
Harmondsworth, Middlesex, England

First published in 1991 by Viking Penguin,
a division of Penguin Books USA Inc.

10 9 8 7 6 5 4 3 2 1

LIBRARY OF CONGRESS CATALOGING IN PUBLICATION DATA
Schutz, Benjamin M.
    A fistful of empty / Benjamin M. Schutz.
      p.   cm.
    ISBN 0-670-83111-5
    I. Title.
    PS3569.C5556F57   1991
    813'.54—dc20   90-50340

Printed in the United States of America
Set in Times Roman

The briefer the spell, the more potent the magic.

ACKNOWLEDGMENTS

I would like to thank the following people for the gracious donation of their expertise: Howard Miller and Christi Cherry of Howard Miller & Associates Detective Agency; Fred W. Frank and Barry Udoff of Fred W. Frank Bail Bondsman, Inc.; David Karrick of Dean, Witter Reynolds; Mark Schutz, M.D., and Officer Adam Schutz, MPDC; and especially Neil Ruther and Lew Read.

The Last Dance

The cock crows
The strings grow silent
And the ballroom lights
Burn out;
The Dancers
Grow old and wrinkled,
Die and are gone—
And winds blow—
Dust in the corners.

—Melvin Schutz (1924–1989)

A FISTFUL
OF EMPTY

1

No doubt about it, Charlie Babcock had spit right in my eye.
A nice thick one to boot.

I pushed back from my desk and spun around in my chair.
Round and round I went like a dog checking out its bed. I slid
my new glasses up onto my forehead and rubbed my eyes.
Nothing worked, the cases were still there. I had given them
one last chance to take wing and they had obstinately refused.
Who did they think I was, Harry S. Truman? I looked at my
watch. Two prime Saturday night hours gone, shot, pissed away,
and nothing to show for them except some freshly sharpened
pencils and a notepad that now sported hospital corners.

I took a deep breath, adjusted my glasses, and stacked the
case files in ascending order of awful. Three weeks ago I'd fired
Babcock for falsifying expense vouchers. Since then, he'd contacted every person he'd had under surveillance and told them
who was watching them and why. No doubt he'd vastly im-
proved on our severance package. I let him go with just a
busted lip.

I read each file and made notes for the report the owner of
the agency, Rocky Franklin, had requested. Damage control,
he called it. Among other things.

First up was Samuel Yates, last address a steam grate near

Union Station. Sam was heir to $700,000 from his grandfather's estate. Babcock had contacted him first, costing us our expenses in locating him and our finder's fee. Pure spite that one, and a total loss.

Next was Ricky Zingone, whiplash victim and 4-handicap golfer. Babcock had gone with the roll of film immortalizing Ricky's scintillating 71 at Pine Crest. What form, what follow-through. And only a week after the accident. Ricky was now in a brace and a wheelchair. Dominion Insurance terminated their contract with us immediately. I recommended to Rocky that we reopen negotiations with them on a trial basis in six months. Their damage-control report would be deeply filed by then and they might be able to remember our previous track record for them.

Then there was Beverly Grimes. She was no longer leaving eighteen-month-old Rodney alone at night so she could go looking for love in all the wrong places. Her history said that she wouldn't be able to keep that up for more than three weeks. I recommended continuing the surveillance at our expense, and made a note to call Rodney's father first thing in the morning.

Dr. Ahmed Naboukian was the fourth of Babcock's going-away presents. He had taken a sudden vacation to Brazil. Closed the office, kissed the wife, and poof!, he turned into the toad he really was. The bastard wouldn't be doing any more gynecological exams with his one-eyed viper, not in the States anyway. Brazil was going to be a big problem though, since it has no extradition treaty with the United States. Ahmed must have read that in the travel brochure when he was looking for a new swamp to jump into. I suggested assembling our clients and introducing them to Mrs. Mona Naboukian. Perhaps that would convince her to help lure his toadhood out of Brazil to a locale where he could be boxed up and returned to face charges. If not, then I recommended moving immediately to file charges and attempt to freeze his assets before she could assist him in liquidating them and funneling them into a Brazilian bank.

Last there was Jack Carruthers, wanted for snatching his daughter Crystal, age four, from her mother. Jack felt unjustly constrained by the "absurd" court order requiring supervised visitation. He claimed that he was "liberating" Crystal from her "brainwashing" mother. All that aside, Jack did not also have a good explanation for the video he'd sold Charlie of him sodomizing little Crystal. We got lucky with Jack and didn't lose him when he suddenly broke cover and hopped a plane to Atlanta. I called Crystal's mother to explain what had happened and that we still had her husband under surveillance. She slammed the phone down so hard that when I called back I was told it was out of service. An hour later, her lawyer called to tell me that Hagberg & Associates were now handling the case and that if I sent any bill at all to Ms. Toomey, he'd add three zeroes to the damages on the lawsuit he was preparing. I respectfully advised Rocky that we eat shit on this case and politely ask for seconds.

Our lawyers had good news and bad news for us. The good news was that we could sue Babcock for breach of contract. The bad news was that the people he'd informed would have to testify against him to prove that he'd betrayed us. I told Rocky that I thought we'd have more luck opening up an ACLU office in Tehran.

I further noted that we should file a grievance with the state licensing board and the local investigators' associations. I had already met privately with colleagues and standing just this side of slander had pissed into every watering hole he might visit.

I scanned the report one last time and closed by tendering my resignation.

It looked like old Charlie was going to get away with it. This time, anyway. He'd hurt us and our clients a lot worse than we could hurt him. But someday, somewhere, our paths would cross again. At least I hoped so.

I locked my desk and turned off the lights. The files and report I put in my secretary's IN box. I was almost out the door when the phone rang. I reached across the receptionist's desk to pick it up.

"Hello."

"Leo, what are you doing in the office?" It was Samantha, claimed by all who know me to be my better half.

"Cleaning up after Charlie Babcock, that's what. Where are you?"

"Home. I couldn't take another minute in New York. I felt battered the entire time I was there." She sighed. "I don't know what it is. Maybe it's me. New York used to be exciting and glamorous. This time it felt like a feeding frenzy, people just flaying each other. It felt raw. Raw and awful. A gigantic boiling stew of desperation."

"Did anything happen to you?"

"No. I was insulated from all that. Chauffered limos, maitre'd's and bellboys between me and the city. Like some kind of reverse zoo, where the ones behind bars are the lucky ones. But I felt like I had no skin at all, no boundaries, everything just went right through me."

This didn't surprise me. Lately Sam had been chronically moody. Unfortunately her range only went from the merely cranky to the totally crazed. I thought it was because her writing wasn't going well, but she refused to discuss that with me. I kept a low profile these days, figuring that it would pass, as all storms do, and hoping that part of the aftermath would be some understanding for both of us.

"When will you be home?" she asked.

"Not for a while."

"Do you have more work to do?" A trace of whine set in.

"No. I've done what I can about Charlie Babcock. I have a meeting with Arnie tonight."

"Can't it wait?" Annoyed now.

"No, it can't. I'm helping him with a job." Equally annoyed, I sank to the occasion.

"What kind of job?"

"A bounty-hunting job."

"Why are you doing that? You said you weren't going to be working the streets anymore. Why not let the police back him up?"

I closed my eyes. I hated to visualize Samantha when she sounded like this. Wearily, I started with the simplest question, "Because the police won't help him. It pisses them off that he gets the money he does for doing the same job they do, bringing in the bad guys. Besides that, he's embarrassed them a couple of times. They'd love to see him take a fall."

"So, let somebody from the agency do it. Assign somebody. Isn't that your job?"

Well, fuck you too. "Yes, it is. But you know Arnie. He doesn't trust anyone but me."

"So, what does that mean? When we're on our honeymoon, if Arnie calls, I get to finish by myself?"

"Whoa, whoa, what's the big deal here? I'll be out for"—I checked my watch—"another couple of hours, maybe three at the most. Then I'm home."

"Leo, I really want you to come home now. It's important. There are things we have to talk about."

"Fine. So let's talk. What is it?" I knew I was being an asshole.

"Not over the phone."

"Why not?" I wasn't sure I wanted to know. The way she'd been acting recently, I couldn't envision good news.

"I can't believe I have to explain myself to you. I said it's important, Leo, isn't that enough?"

"Well, I'm sorry, Sam. Most of the time you don't. But tonight, I told Arnie that I'd back him up and he's counting on me." Nothing. "Sam, he's my friend."

"And what does that make me?" she asked, hanging up before I could reply, although truth be known, I wasn't sure what I would have said.

2

Arnie and I parked two blocks away from the address he had for Harold "Warthog" Snipes. Arnie had disconnected the car's interior lights, so I used a flashlight to read the file on Snipes. Single; twenty years old; no fixed address; no visible means of support; driver's license suspended; only nearby relative was his mother, Hilda Snipes; dropped out of the tenth grade. I skimmed the juvenile history of increasingly serious offenses met by increasingly futile sanctions. At seventeen, Harold had joined the Fourth Reich, where he now held the rank of Uberschutzmann, which was probably pidgin German for doltschmuck.

I flipped to the picture and description. The biggest mistake a bounty hunter can make is to bring in the wrong man. Then you're just a kidnapper. Last year Arnie had pissed off the cops big time when he brought in the right Burgess twin. Seems they hadn't taken the time to read the twins' medical records and check for scars. Bringing in the wrong twin might not have been considered negligence except that the lawyer subpoenaed Arnie to explain how he managed to get it right. The settlement was for the legendary "undisclosed amount." The result for Arnie was that he was on an unofficial blacklist. There was no police backup for him at any time.

I slipped the picture out for a closer look. Snipes's egg-shaped head was completely shaved. In the center of his forehead he had commissioned a work of art: a swastika. No going back now, Harold. His complexion was pale and pockmarked on the cheeks. Between his blue-gray eyes, his snout was broad and upturned. The dark, round nostrils were like the twin barrels of a shotgun and just as pleasant to look up. His smile was a thing to behold and the obvious source of his nickname. The jutting underlip and the wide gap between his canines made them look just like tusks.

All of this beauty was perched upon a six foot three, 317-pound walking landfill that favored steel-toed boots, blue jeans and suspenders, and white T-shirts. In addition to his hood ornament he had the twin lightning bolts and skull of the S.S. on the outside of each bicep and wore large rings on each finger, creating legal brass knuckles.

"How'd you find this monstrosity?" I asked.

Arnie smiled. "Passed some money around. A couple of people have met Harold and not been charmed."

"What are we bringing him in for?"

"He was the wheelman for that drive-by killing in George-town, when they hit that rabbi last fall."

"Yeah, right after Yom Kippur services let out."

"You got it."

"What's the price on him?"

"Bail was two hundred thousand. I get ten percent plus expenses. The synagogue has tacked on a twenty-five thousand reward, another fifty for the shooter."

"Really?"

"Yeah. I don't think they liked it when Harold said 'What's the beef? He was in season.' "

"How long did it take you to find him?"

"Not long. A couple of weeks. Snipes is a creature of habit, a real 'gashhound.' Just had to find his current honey and watch her. Why do you ask?"

"I sent Rocky Franklin my resignation tonight."

"Over the Babcock thing?"

"Yeah."

"Don't you think that was a little extreme?"

"Maybe, but I don't think I can assume that he'll want me to stay on after this fiasco."

"So it's vote of confidence time?"

"Right. And if it's a no, then I need a fallback position. Maybe bounty hunting is it."

"We've come full circle, haven't we, Leo?"

I nodded. "Yeah, I guess we have."

"How long did I work for you?"

"I don't know that it was for me, I always thought it was with me. Ten years, I guess."

"Well, if Rocky dumps you, which would surprise me, you can fall back to this. I'm getting much bigger jobs than you could command right away. Besides it'd be fun, you and me working together again."

"Thanks, Arnie. Part of me hopes that Rocky does can me. And if he does, this'll beat the hell out of unemployment. Maybe Sam'll see it that way when I talk to her."

"Check the papers on Snipes, would you, Leo? I want to be able to dump him tonight."

"Right." I made sure that we had copies of the letter of employment from the bail bondsman, the bail agreement, the notice of forfeiture, and the bench warrant. Together they constituted our legal right to act as the jailers of Harold Snipes wherever he might be found.

"Everything's there."

"You ready to go, Leo?"

"Let's do it."

We pulled up a couple of blocks until we were catty-corner to Snipes's hideout.

"When his honey goes to work, we'll make our move."

"What does she do?" I asked. "Going to work at this time."

"She dances bottomless at a club on Georgia Avenue."

About twenty minutes later the girl trotted down the stairs, got into a car, and drove off. Arnie rolled forward across the intersection, past the alley behind the house, and made a right turn at the next corner. When we were directly behind the house, Arnie slowed a bit and I jumped out and ran between the houses toward the alley and Snipes's backyard.

Arnie continued up to the end of the block and turned right. I saw him paralleling me as I crossed the alley. If our timing was right, he'd glide silently in front of the house ten seconds after I had finished with the back steps.

I ran in a crouch across the backyard and squatted next to the stairs leading down from the back porch. I didn't feature the "Warthog" vaulting any railings, not at 317 pounds. So if he went out the back, he'd have to go down the stairs. I wrapped the 130-pound fishing line around one upright, taped it into place, and ran it across to the other post. When it was secured, I checked the tension. It should hit him mid-shin. Face up or face down, he wouldn't be hard to find.

I scuttled alongside the building to the bushes at the front left corner. Arnie pulled up in front of the house. He had coasted down with the engine off. Braking to a halt, he slid out of the driver's side and ran toward the front door. He was dressed like me, entirely in black, and when he moved he was just a ripple in the night.

On the front porch, we pulled out our guns. We were using light loads because the house was a duplex. The last thing we wanted were slugs going through the walls and hitting the neighbors.

I pulled out my flashlight and held it high and away from my body. Arnie would go in first.

The house plans we'd reviewed showed a kitchen door in the back left side and a bathroom under the head of the staircase going up the right wall.

Fortunately there wasn't a screen door. Arnie looked at me. I nodded. The door opened on the left. I crossed to the left side and kept the flashlight in my right hand. Arnie crouched down to the level of the knob. He turned it slowly. It was unlocked and he pushed it open. Snipes should go in for being criminally stupid. I flashed the light around the room, hitting the doors and the top of the stairs, then turned it off. In that instant Arnie crossed into the room and stood against the left wall. I crossed behind him, reached back with my left elbow, and pushed the door closed. I nudged it with my ass until the lock clicked.

The bathroom was first. Arnie and I crossed to the door and repeated our synchronized flash-and-move sequence. Nothing. When Arnie closed the door, I put a strip of black tape across the edge. If Snipes got behind us and hid in a room we'd already checked, he'd dislodge the tape and give himself away. At least that's the theory.

The kitchen was empty. I taped the door and we moved to the staircase. Going up a staircase after a jumper is like making Pickett's charge knowing how it turned out.

According to the plans, the second floor had a bathroom door at the top of the stairs and two bedrooms on the left side of the hall. Each bedroom had a closet and the bathroom tub probably had a shower curtain. Six more doors. I took a deep breath and nodded at Arnie. It would be like this until we found Snipes. Coiling in readiness outside each doorway, riding the waves of adrenalin that rolled through, then making our move just before excitement crested and fell into fear.

We went up the stairs. My jaws ached and my eyes were dry and scratchy. Halfway up the stairs, I swung in an arc toward the bedroom doors. Arnie stood outside the bathroom door. There was no way that I could give him any light and cover his back. He was on his own. Both bedroom doors were closed. Arnie squatted down and pushed the bathroom door open. He went through. Silence. I imagined him pulling back the shower curtain. Hello Norman Bates. Blessed silence.

Arnie came back out. I climbed the rest of the stairs and

taped the door. Four left. Arnie put his ear to the first door and shook his head. We went to the second door. This time Arnie signaled uncertainty. If he was right, we were done, if not, Snipes would be alerted and behind us. I shook my head no. We backed away from the door.

Then it came upon us. A combination snore and whistle, chased by a shudder. Arnie and I grinned and tiptoed back to the front bedroom. Had to be the "Warthog" dreaming of a romp on the veldt.

I stood behind Arnie, squatting with his hand on the knob. I had my flashlight ready and tapped him on the head with my gun hand. At the silent count of three, he opened the door. Flash and move and we were in.

There, on a mattress on the floor, was Harold Snipes. Face down, his blubbery lips flapped with each snore. One huge arm hung off the mattress onto the floor. Fortunately, he was fully dressed. All we had to do was wake him up and wrap him to go.

I scanned the room. The closet was open. Arnie kept his gun on Snipes. I backed out and went to check the other bedroom. It was empty. When I returned, Arnie took a position at Snipes's feet. I stood by his outstretched arm. That way there wouldn't be any chance of an accidental crossfire if Snipes did something suicidal. I shone the light in his eyes as Arnie kicked him in the leg.

Snipes threw his arm up in front of his eyes and rolled onto his side. "What the fuck?" he snarled.

He put his arm down and stopped blinking. His eyes jumped back and forth between our guns. "Oh shit. Who are you guys? What do you want?"

"Shut up, lardass," I snapped, and asked Arnie, "Is he the one?"

"I don't know. He sure looks like him, though. What's your name, Fats?"

Snipes was silent.

Arnie shook his head. "You're pissing me off, Fats. I don't get paid if I kill the wrong guy, but I might just do you for the practice."

Snipes squinted at us. He was cataloguing his sins, trying to figure out which ones were worth killing him for.

"You the Jews?"

"Shit." Arnie chuckled. "Do we look like the fucking Jews?"

Snipes pondered that for a second, then he smiled. "Harold Snipes, that's my name."

"Gotcha, scumbag. We're from the Ace Bonding Company," Arnie said.

"Oh shit," Snipes whined and started to get up.

Arnie centered his gun on the swastika on Harold's forehead and said, "Face down, Snipes. Put your arms out, palms up. Turn your head away and no talking."

"Shit, Harold, what were you expecting, guys with horns on their heads?" I asked.

Snipes did as he was told. Arnie holstered his gun, took his handcuffs out of his pocket, and flipped them open. He locked one around Snipes's left wrist, twisted the arm, and bent it back like a chicken wing. He reached over and grabbed the right wrist and pulled it back toward the open cuff. It wouldn't reach.

"Jesus Christ, Snipes, what did you do, eat the Fourth Reich?" he asked, then stepped away from him. "Roll up to a sit, Snipes. Cross your legs underneath you. Raise your hands overhead."

I watched Snipes follow the commands. When he sat up, his chest sank and flattened against the uppermost terrace of his belly. Three more folds bulged against his T-shirt. The lower deck covered half of his thighs. I wasn't worried about handcuffing him anymore. If he went limp on us, we'd need a winch to get him into the car.

Arnie snapped the cuffs around Snipes's right wrist. "Keep your arms up," he said.

Arnie stepped around in front of him. "All right, put your hands in front of you. Lean forward, putting your weight on your hands. Uncross your legs. Now get up, one leg at a time."

Snipes moved ponderously, dutifully executing each command. Together they looked like a circus act: Arnie Kendall and his trunkless elephant, Harold. Once he was on his feet, Arnie guided him toward the wall. Two or three feet away he grabbed Harold's belt.

"Keep your hands down," he barked. Slowly Arnie leaned him forward until his forehead touched the wall. He kicked his legs apart so that Harold was precariously balanced and then frisked him. He was clean.

"All right, Harold, let's go." Arnie straightened him up and pointed him at the door. I flipped off the light.

On the stairs, I snuck a look at my watch. We'd been inside for twenty-two minutes. Not bad, not bad at all. Another twenty minutes to the station house, five maybe ten to dump Harold, another twenty back to my car, and I could call it a night.

Arnie guided Harold around the bottom of the stairs toward the front door. My gun was still in the middle of his back. A slice of light crossed the floor toward us. I followed it back to its source.

Arnie's head snapped right and he reached for his gun as a shape tore itself loose from the wall. The gun waving wildly under his nose convinced him to stop. "Don't move!" she shouted.

"Awright," Snipes cheered huskily.

I rammed my gun into his back and grabbed his waistband. "Hold it, Harold."

Even though the girl held the gun with both hands, the pistol was bouncing like a seismograph. I stepped away from behind Arnie, keeping my gun in Harold's back.

"Let him go!" she yelled.

"No," Arnie said, flat and cold.

"You'd better, or I'll blow your fucking head off," she snapped. Ah, true love.

"So? My partner kills Harold right here. In fact, where he's standing now, his .45 goes straight through Harold and blows you away, too. That purse gun you're holding isn't going to kill anyone. You know that. When you bought it, you told the guy you just wanted something to scare people with, right?"

In the darkness, I couldn't see her eyes. No way to read how she was going to play it. Arnie adjusted his stance a bit and I saw him move his arm slightly away from his side.

"Maybe so, but I can't miss from here."

"Sure you can. Look at your hands. You're all over the place. You've never fired this piece, you don't know what the recoil is like. You're probably going to shoot Harold there."

This whole thing was going to hell. I knew Arnie. There was no way this little girl and her peashooter were going to back him off of Snipes's carcass.

The girl and Arnie were locked in a staredown. She might have the gun, but he was the cat and she was the mouse. Arnie would be watching the barrel bouncing around, settling into a rhythm, not even seeing her at all, just the gun. Getting loose, then focused, then ready.

Four sets of eyes on that damned gun. What was she going to do? My chest felt like I was breathing cement.

She flicked her eyes away from Arnie. "Harold?"

Arnie's arm flew up and his hand clamped over the cylinder. She pulled the trigger but the cylinder wouldn't rotate. Arnie twisted the gun away from his body and butted her right in the face.

The girl let out a groan and crumpled with her hand to her face. Arnie stepped to the side, twisted her arm until her fingers opened up, and pulled the gun out of her grasp. He stepped over her and walked to the back of the house.

I looked down. She was curled up on her side, crying, with both hands held to her face.

"Your girlfriend, Harold?"

"Yeah," he grunted.

"What made you come back?"

She didn't answer.

"You've got guts, I'll give you that."

"Fuck that, she had the drop on him," Harold complained.

"Hell, Harold, is that your idea of comfort?"

Arnie came back. He bent over and handed a towel to the girl. "Keep that on your face. It's full of ice. It'll keep the swelling down. You've still got to work."

Snipes and I followed Arnie out of the house. Behind me I heard the girl mutter, "Fuck you."

3

We hustled Harold out to the car. I swear he grew and the car shrank, the closer we got. Arnie pulled open the back door and Harold laughed at him.

"You can't put me in there. There ain't enough room."

I shook my head. We might as well try to put a walrus in a change purse.

Arnie looked into the car and then back at Harold. He pressed his lips together, then shook his head.

"You'll fit. It won't be fun, but you'll fit."

"Arnie, are you sure? This isn't origami, you know. No matter how you fold him, he's still 317 pounds of shit."

"He'll fit."

"Fuck this, I ain't movin'."

Arnie spun and slipped him the old two-finger comealong. Ram your fingers two knuckles deep in a man's nose and threaten to make a fist. He'll follow you anywhere.

Arnie led him to the door. "Let's go, Harold, put your ass on the seat. Now your left leg in. Tuck your head down, further."

"I can't. I can't breathe," he rasped.

Arnie reached in and jammed Harold's head past the doorframe. He popped up inside like a righted buoy. I heard something rip. It was the seam on his jeans.

"Now your right leg. Attaboy."

Harold was in, seated in the center of the back seat with his legs splayed to support his belly and his hands in front of him. Arnie unrolled a chain attached to the door frame, looped it between Harold's cuffed fists, pulled it tight to the other side of the car, and padlocked it.

We got in the front and Arnie spoke to Harold as he turned on the ignition.

"Be good, Harold. If you make a ruckus and we have an accident, there's no way you'll get out ahead of a fire. Understand?"

"Fuck you."

We let the pleasantry pass and headed over to district headquarters.

With a couple of uneventful minutes under my belt I began to relax. Slowly each muscle group stood down from red alert. I took a deep breath and tried to expel my fear.

We sped along in the dark and I rolled down the window to feel the night breeze on my face. I tried to sort out why I had put myself in such jeopardy. Like a pinball game, my mind caromed off a number of answers, each one lighting up briefly, then sending me on to another. Each answer I found was plausible. None was compelling.

I'd given Arnie my word. We were friends. I hated my job. I still wanted to be on the streets. I wasn't that old. I couldn't stand to just take it from Charlie Babcock. I had to do something to somebody. And on and on. They all seemed so important until I got to the part where that wild-eyed girl was waving a gun in my face. Then they all winked out and I had no answer at all. Just dumb luck to get me through. That and Arnie's reflexes.

"You ever pull that stunt before?" I asked.

"Not live, no. But I practice it all the time."

"And how often do you make it?"

"Two out of ten, I'd say."

"Two out of ten. Did I hear that right, two out of ten?"

"Uh-huh."

"Jesus, Arnie, what made you try it?"

"She looked like one of the two."

"Uh-huh, right, that's it? She just looked ripe for the old one-handed snake-in-the-dark cylinder jam."

"It worked. I must have been right."

"I guess. I guess." I closed my eyes and shook my head in disbelief. A tremor passed through me, a sickening shockwave of recognition. I'd just bent down to kiss the ground beneath my feet and found only a high wire there. I clutched the door handle reflexively until my vertigo passed, and then felt foolish.

Snipes belched as a preamble, then said, "Look, guys, can't we cut a deal here?"

When he got no reply, he went on, "I mean, if you ain't the Jews, then this is just business, right? What am I worth to you guys, twenty grand?"

"Forty-five," Arnie said. "The Jews put twenty-five on you themselves."

"Fuckers. Hell, it doesn't matter. I can turn you onto something worth a lot more. A whole lot more."

"Right, Harold. All of a sudden you're a Donald Trump."

"No, it's true. Let me go and I'll show you something worth a fortune."

I found Harold's face in the rear-view mirror. "Harold, don't take this personally, but I haven't seen you on 'Lifestyles of the Rich and Famous.' You'll have to tell us a little something more about this treasure you've got."

"All right, I can dig it. Okay?"

I turned to face Harold. He was positively glowing, irradiated with hope.

"It's drugs, man. Big time. Millions maybe. That's what I got. What do you say we cut a deal?"

"Sounds interesting, Harold. Tell us more."

"No way. We cut a deal. Then I talk."

Arnie and I looked at each other. I factored in Harold's situation, his track record on all the major virtues, and the consequences of getting all slimy with him. He got no in stereo.

"Well, fuck you, you Jew-loving, nigger-fucking . . ."

Arnie turned the wheel hard to the right and slammed on the brakes. Slowly he turned around in his seat.

"Harold, I get paid for bringing you in. It doesn't say in one piece, or even in good condition. Just alive. It seems to me that you're in no position to piss me off. Now put a lid on it or you'll get a chance to meet some of them Jews you're so fond of. You understand me?"

For the rest of the ride, Harold was a good boy.

At the station house, Arnie and I unwrapped our prizewinner. He unlocked the chain and fed it between Harold's fists onto the floor of the back seat.

I told Harold to lay down on his side, roll over onto his stomach, and wriggle feet first out of the car. He moved like a python with a hernia.

I got back in the car and watched Arnie march him up the front steps. I just wanted to go home and go to bed. Modest goals, I thought.

4

At home, I quietly unlocked the door and tiptoed inside. The house was dark and still. Feeling my way along the walls, I went back to the bedroom. I stopped outside the door and listened for Sam's breathing but heard nothing. I gripped the knob and slowly turned it. It wouldn't move. I tried again. Locked. I stepped back, puzzled. My eyes adjusted to the darkness and I saw something on the door. I reached up and grabbed it. Paper. I pulled it off the door and went back to the kitchen where I flipped on the light over the sink. It was a note to me. I leaned back against the counter and read it.

Leo—
If I had anyplace else to go, I'd be there. But I don't, so please don't try to get in. I don't want to be close to you, and I'm too upset even to fight. I don't seem to be able to reach you anymore. Maybe this will.

My first thought was whether to honor the note. Maybe it was a test and I should kick the door in to prove something. Even as tired and muddled as I was, that seemed clearly stupid. Sam had never been one for sleight-of-heart tricks. The geometry of her desires was all straight lines. Then again, I could always kick the door in because this was just so much bullshit.

Instead I paced aimlessly through the kitchen, opened the refrigerator and poked through things, grazing without hunger. I walked out to the living room, sat down, and kicked off my shoes. Getting undressed seemed way too complicated. I moved over into my easy chair, leaned back, and began to spin in a slow circle. My chair finally stopped, facing the utter blackness of the house. Denied action, I did the only other thing I'm any good at—I brooded. But every question I delivered was stillborn.

Sometime before dawn I fell asleep. When I awoke it seemed only an instant had passed. I sat up staring at my hands, certain that I had dropped something, that it had slipped right through my fingers. I shook off the feeling and walked back to the bedroom. Samantha was gone. This time there was no note.

5

Sam was gone all day. I know because I called home every hour, left a message for her to call me, and retrieved them all, unplayed, at five o'clock.

I went to work but should have gone to the moon instead. I doodled and called, then doodled and called again. I went out for lunch and ate nothing. I came back, read case files, and remembered nothing. Kelly, my secretary, came in to tell me that I looked like hell and should go home so she could stop worrying about me and get some of her work done. It was almost the least that I could do and so I managed it.

Sam was in the kitchen when I got home. There was no smile, no hello when I came in. I thought better of trying to kiss her and settled for a beer. She moved like a zombie, making dinner by rote. Her face was a mask with eyes as soft as marbles.

"How long are we going to do this?" I asked, eager for a fight, for anything.

"Do what?" she said, slashing me with her indifference.

"Oh, cut the shit, Sam, you know what I mean. There's a dead moose right here between us and it stinks to hell. When are we going to do something about it?"

She put down the knife she was cutting the tomatoes with and picked at a stray piece on the counter.

"I don't know."

"Well, take a guess. We've got nothing on tap."

"I told you, I don't know."

"Well, that doesn't cut it. So I went out with Arnie and didn't come running when you called. What's the big fucking deal? What is it that couldn't wait? I'm right here."

"Forget it. I don't want to talk to you."

"Yeah, and you don't want to sleep with me, either. What do you want, anyway?" Move over Sigmund and everybody else.

"I told you a long time ago. It's no mystery."

God, I hate pop quizzes. I flipped through the operations manual on Samantha Clayton.

"What? You're not number one in my life?"

"That'll do for starters."

"Jesus Christ, Sam, what do you want? To be joined at the hip? I told you why I did it. I'm not going to jump every time you say boo."

"I didn't say boo. I told you that it was important and that I needed you then. That just didn't make it. So, fine, I know where I stand."

Yeah, all day in the sun without a hat, that's where. "Sam, you're making a mountain out of a molehill. Nothing's changed that I can see."

"Oh, that's where you're wrong, Leo, everything has changed."

"So tell me about it."

"No. I'm still thinking about it. When I've decided, I'll tell you."

"Gee, thanks. Well, you know where to find me."

I drained the beer and thought about another six as chasers. Boy, talking to her was fun. We should do it more often.

I told no one in particular that I was going out for a while and left to a round of silence. I was amazed at how badly that had gone. The night before, I'd concluded that my life with Sam was worth more than all the reasons I'd had for going with Arnie. How come that was the one thing I hadn't said?

That question stuck in my mind like a "Tilt" sign. Was it really true? What did we really have going for us? More useless fights like this? No. There was more there. This was some aberration, an increasingly frequent one, but still an aberration. I was convinced of that, maybe. I would wait her out and see what she had to say.

I reached that conclusion somewhere out near Culpeper and it took me almost an hour to get back home.

6

Sam broke her silence around four the next afternoon and called me at the office. I told her that I'd be right home and that if traffic was bad, I'd call her from the car with an estimate of the delay. She didn't hang up with a kiss, but it was a start.

I left our office in Old Town, Alexandria, and made my way to the Beltway. Traffic crossing the Woodrow Wilson Bridge was at a halt and backing up like toppling dominoes.

The Beltway is permanently under construction. They have a secret formula that balances any expansion against the growth in traffic so that when the construction is complete it is at least as inadequate to the traffic flows as when they first began the work. Then they approve more work and it goes back under construction.

Traffic had clotted at "The Split" where I-95, 495, and 395 converge and fifteen lanes split, braid, collapse, and emerge as four each going east-west and north-south. The numbering system to guide you through this is incomprehensible to anyone without a learning disability.

I crept through the concrete terraces that climbed the sky. When I called Sam, the line was busy. Eventually I exited at Route 50 and Gallows Road, then turned off Gallows and zigzagged to my house. Sam's car was in the driveway.

I climbed out, an unstable mix of yearning and apprehension, and walked to the front door. It was open. That silly potato head. I pushed it back. "Sam, I'm ho . . . ," I started to say.

The living room had been trashed. Furniture tossed and slashed, bookshelves emptied onto the floor. I squatted inside the door and drew my pistol. Then I peeked around the kitchen's half-counter and scanned the room. No one. No legs sticking out from behind the sofa, no pools of blood.

At a silent "three," I popped up over the counter, a homicidal Jack-in-the-box, and pointed my gun around the kitchen. No one there. Just food and broken glassware all over the floor, and the one beer bottle on the counter. Back in the box, I duckwalked around the corner to the bedroom and my office.

My office door was open and the chaos continued inside. Papers were everywhere, file drawers yanked out and dumped. The carpet had been pulled back to reveal the floor safe. It was still closed. Sam didn't know the combination. Hadn't wanted to. Ignorance is bliss, she'd said. So nonchalant, so long ago.

I turned and faced the bathroom. The door was open. I could see everything but the toilet in the corner. He could be standing on it. No choice. I sprang into the center of the room, gun up, and almost shot myself in the mirror.

The bedroom door was closed. I put my ear to it and heard nothing. I took a step back and crushed my fears between clenched teeth. Coming through. The door slammed back.

Sam was on the bed, bound and hooded, a pool of blood between her legs. I pulled the hood off. A thin belt of hers was around her throat. I followed it back to one of the bedposts, unknotted it, and slid the noose over her head. A livid bruise remained. Her mouth was taped shut. As gently as I could, I peeled the tape off. She was rigid from the waist up and arched, with her head thrown back. I rolled her onto her side, pulled out my knife, and cut the plastic ties around her wrists.

I called her name quietly. She said nothing. I searched her face. Her eyes were stretched wide and empty. Panicked, I checked her breathing. She was alive but in shock. Bruises mottled her arms and legs. I pulled up a sheet and covered her.

"I'm going to call an ambulance, Sam. I'll be right back."

I ran from the room, found the phone, and dialed 911. As I spoke, I watched my right hand tremble and shake. It was curious, that's all, just curious, not being my hand, of course. I put the phone down.

This was somebody else's life. I was sure of that. I only had to stay here until they returned to claim it. Then I was out of here.

7

I followed the ambulance to the hospital. In its wake, I ran every light. "Just let her live, Lord," I thought. "I can work with anything I get after that." It was a lie and we both knew it. I asked for it, anyway.

At the emergency entrance, they backed the ambulance up to a loading dock. Two nurses were standing there. I had told the paramedics everything I knew and they had radioed the information ahead to the emergency room.

I pulled up next to the ambulance, clambered out of the car, and hopped up the stairs to the loading area. The ambulance was open and they were sliding Sam out. She had an IV in her arm and a nasal tube for oxygen. Her eyes seemed clearer as they darted back and forth. I reached for her hand and squeezed it. It stayed soft in my grip. I felt a hand on my elbow.

"I'm sorry, but you can't come in here," a voice said, firmly and evenly.

I turned and glared. It was one of the nurses. I stared at her long-jawed Nordic face: blond curls, blue eyes, pale skin, no makeup, thin lips, no smile.

"Why the hell not? Look at her, she's terrified."

"I know that. But we can't do anything for her until you leave. You can't do anything for her in there."

I shook myself free. "Yes I can. She's frightened. She doesn't know what's going to happen to her. She's been through enough. I can help keep her calm."

"Perhaps, but who's going to keep you calm? You don't know what we might have to do. It's difficult enough caring for her, we can't be distracted by having to deal with you."

Sam was rolling away, through swinging doors, out of sight. I leaned forward. The nurse put her hand on my chest.

"If you really care for her, let us do our jobs. Please, go into the waiting room. We can't do anything for her until you go. It's up to you."

Her words seeped into me, leaching my resolve.

"All right," I said, and stepped around her toward the waiting-room doors.

I slammed through and was stalking past the admitting desk when a voice said, "Sir."

"Yes," I snapped.

"Did you bring someone into the emergency room?"

"Yes."

"Then you'll have to fill out these forms." The woman held out a clipboard to me. I felt like flipping it out of her hand. She looked tired. I took the clipboard. She hadn't done anything to me.

I walked over to an empty corner, sat down, and checked the time. Minute one was 5:47. I scanned the form and began to fill in the blanks. At marital status, I paused. Lovers have no rights. I wanted to know how she was doing. So, I listed Sam as married and identified myself as her husband. That done, I just kept lying. In my new role I gave permissions, signed releases, and promised payment. Hell, if you're skating on thin ice you might as well dance.

I killed ten minutes on the paperwork, turned it in, and returned to my seat. Time passed like a kidney stone. I tried to think about what had happened. Was the rape the intended crime or an afterthought to a robbery? What were they looking for? Were they looking for anything at all? Maybe trashing the place was just spite. I couldn't find any answers. Sam's face and her wild empty eyes loomed up behind every question. I had seen that look once before. On a safari, Rocky Franklin and I came upon a zebra surrounded by a pack of hunting dogs. They'd run her to exhaustion. She was frozen, eyes ready to explode, nostrils flaring, spittle hanging from her lips while the dogs ate her alive. They tore chunks of flesh from her flanks, trying to topple her so that the rest of the pack could have at her.

We raised our rifles and fired. I killed three dogs. Rocky killed the zebra. We looked at each other in surprise. The hot savannah wind fanned my face. I squinted into it.

"Excuse me, Mr. Haggerty?"

Startled, I turned to see a burly man standing over me.

"Yes?"

"I'm Detective Rhodasson. Melvin Rhodasson. I'd like to ask you some questions, if I could. I know this is a tough time for you, but the sooner we can get on this the better chance we have of catching whoever did this."

"I'd like to see some I.D. first."

"Sure."

Rhodasson reached into his jacket, pulled out his identification case, and flipped it open. I checked the picture and memorized his badge number.

"Okay, what do you want to know?"

Rhodasson sat down facing me and patted himself, looking for a notepad. While he did that I rewound the tape in my mind, back to the second I approached the door.

Rhodasson found his pad and pen. Pleased with himself, he looked up and said, "Just tell me everything you remember. I'll take notes and then if I have any questions, I'll go back to them."

I went over everything from the unlocked door and my search through the ransacked house to finding Sam.

"You got a good eye for details, Mr. Haggerty. What do you do for a living?"

"I'm a private investigator. I run Franklin Investigations."

"Really? You got a business card?"

I took one out of my wallet and handed it to him. Pocketing it, Rhodasson leaned back, took off his thick glasses, and cleaned them on his tie.

"Your wife say anything to you about what happened?"

"No. She was in shock."

"Right. So, what do you think happened?" All of a sudden we were colleagues.

"I don't know."

"No ideas? Maybe this was about you? Something personal. How about somebody who worked for you? An angry employee, an unhappy client? Someone you dug up some dirt on?"

I filed Charlie Babcock away for later. "No, nothing."

"Nothing? That's too bad. If we had a motive that was related to you or your wife in particular, it would help narrow things down quite a bit. If the assailants were strangers that makes it a lot tougher. But you know that. You must have made some enemies somewhere along the way, Mr. Haggerty. All good detectives have enemies." Rhodasson slipped his glasses back on and stroked the ragged mustache that hung over his thick lips.

"Maybe I'm not that good, Detective Rhodasson," I said, refusing to be baited. I didn't care if he thought I was holding out on him.

Rhodasson shook his head slowly and went back to work. "You touch anything inside the house?"

"Just the phone, when I called. And the hood and bonds."

"Tell me about them."

"The hood was one of Sam's sashes. The tape on her mouth was regular adhesive tape for bandages. The plastic tie was the extra large kind for trash bags."

"You bring them down here?"

"No. I left them on the bed."

"When you went through the house, you find anything missing?"

"I didn't stop to check. I have no idea."

"Did it look like they were looking for something in particular or just trying to piss you off?"

"I don't know. Like I said, my only concern was finding my wife and making sure that she was okay. I haven't thought about any of this."

"I understand that, but you know that if we don't get something more from your wife or some good physical evidence, this one is going to stay open a long time. You sure you don't have any ideas?"

"No, I don't. Believe me, if I did, I'd tell you. I want the bastards who did this caught."

"Why'd you say bastards? What makes you think there was more than one?"

"I don't know. Time, I guess. I don't think there was enough time to toss the place, look through things, and attack my wife. Not for one person."

"Okay. I'm going to talk to your wife when the doctors are done with her. If she tells me anything new, I'll run it by you. We're sending a crew over to check out the crime scene. Is the house locked?"

"No. It seemed a little silly to worry about that."

"Yeah. Well, we'll lock up after ourselves. If we find anything useful, I'll call you. Maybe it'll spark an idea, anything."

"Thanks."

Rhodasson stood up and hoisted his pants over his gut. He stroked his stubbly chin, then ran his palm over his balding head.

"Is there something else, Detective?"

"No. I think that's all, Mr. Haggerty." With that, Rhodasson walked over to the doctor standing at the admitting desk.

I watched them shake hands, and talk for a moment. The doctor nodded toward me. Rhodasson nodded in confirmation. I glanced at the clock. Ten of seven. I watched the doctor walk toward me. Trudging? No. Striding? No. His hands were in his

A FISTFUL OF EMPTY

pockets. What did that mean? No furrows in his brow. And of course, no smile. He was well schooled. In a minute, he might change my life like few people ever had. But for him it was just a day at the office. It had to be that way. I knew that.

Paralyzed with understanding, I just sat there watching him bear down on me and felt my old life slip away as light as gossamer.

The doctor sat down and extended his hand. I shook it and waited for him to open his mouth and sentence me. Funny how a doctor enters a waiting room and all the air rushes out.

"Mr. Haggerty, I'm Dr. Plotnick. I examined your wife in the emergency room."

"How is she?" For Christ sakes.

"She's going to be okay, physically."

"What does that mean?" I was strangling with impatience.

"She has substantial bruising on her arms and legs and some internal bleeding. That's from a blunt trauma injury to the abdomen. She thinks the man hit her with his fist, but she was blindfolded and couldn't see.

"These injuries should resolve themselves without further treatment. I'm more concerned about her emotional condition. She's showing many of the early symptoms of what we call Rape Trauma Syndrome. This is perfectly understandable, mind you, considering what she's been through. First the rape, then . . ."

"Then what?" I snapped.

Plotnick inhaled. "She lost the baby. I'm sorry, Mr. Haggerty."

Stunned, I sat back and watched the puzzles of the last few days re-form with this crucial piece in place. Old mysteries were solved and then quickly replaced with new ones.

In the distance, Plotnick droned on. I heard "Spontaneous miscarriage . . . gynecologist . . . twenty-four to forty-eight hours . . . D&C in the afternoon."

I thought about the child we had lost and felt nothing. He was an absent idea, not a hole in my heart.

"Mr. Haggerty?"

Plotnick was gone. A woman sat in his place. She was leaning forward, elbows on her knees, hands clasped.

"Yes?" What now?

"I'm Dr. Berger. Linda Berger, staff psychologist on duty tonight. I'm with the Victim Resource Network."

I nodded. She was a small woman, with short reddish hair that flared out above her ears to a spiky crown. A forelock hung over one eye. Her features were precise and delicate, but she had an aura of intense energy.

"I've spoken with your wife, Mr. Haggerty, and told her about the services we can provide to help her recover from this attack. I wanted to do the same for you. The husbands of rape victims are victims, too. Very often, though, they don't see themselves that way.

"Your wife may be a very different woman for a while as she comes to grips with what has happened to her. These changes can be very hard for husbands to deal with. You don't know what the right thing to do is anymore.

"Also, most husbands feel a lot of responsibility for their wife's recovery. And while it's important to be there for your wife in whatever fashion she may need, you can't ignore yourself. You'll find that this has stirred up powerful feelings inside you that you'll need to talk about . . ."

"You mean like homicidal rage, like finding the mother-fucking bastard that did this and cutting his dick off and feeding it to him? Something like that?"

I got right in her face, eager to prove her every point. Coolly, she went on.

"Mr. Haggerty, here's my card. A spouse support group meets here every Wednesday at eight p.m. I think you could use it. Your wife is the victim of the same rage that just erupted in you. If she senses that in you, that threat of more violence around her, she'll shrink up inside herself and stop talking about her feelings. She'll halt her own healing because she's afraid of what you might do. What kind of help do you think that is?"

Dr. Berger put her card on the coffee table in front of me and stood up. "Think about what I said, Mr. Haggerty. Will you do that?"

I couldn't bring myself to say yes, so I just nodded. Dr. Berger turned and left.

I sat there and stroked my rage: sleek and pure, red-hot and hungry. Easy, easy. Don't waste this on someone who's just handy. Nothing will satisfy like the right man.

The Sicilians say that revenge is a dish best served cold. Now I knew why.

8

A nurse came by and told me that Sam was being taken up to Room 407 and that when she was settled in, I could come up and see her. I asked how long it would take and she said to come up in about ten minutes.

Those last ten minutes crept by slower than the first ten. I paced. I chewed a nail. Then two. I hit the elevator button and hopped from one foot to the other waiting for its arrival. I'd have taken the stairs if I could have found the right ones.

When the elevator arrived, I popped in and hit four. Seconds later I strode through the doors to Wing 4E and began searching for number 407. The nurses glanced at me as I went past their station and then returned to their charting.

I pushed open the door to 407 and peeked in. A nurse was tucking in Sam's blankets. She looked up at me and mouthed "Two minutes." Sam's face was hidden behind a hanging curtain. The other bed in the room was empty.

When the nurse came out, I approached her and asked, "Can I go in now?"

"Yes. She may get a little groggy soon. The doctor gave her some medication for pain."

I nodded. "Can I spend the night here?"

"In her room?"

"Yes."

"No. I'm sorry, but that's not allowed on this ward. Visiting hours are over in about fifteen minutes. You can spend the night in one of the waiting rooms or down in the lobby, but not in her room. The doctor wants her to have a sedative to help her sleep. She'll be getting that pretty soon. You look like you should go home and try to get some sleep."

"Yeah."

I pushed the door open and closed it gently behind me. I approached the bed and pulled back the curtain. Sam looked asleep. There was a chair in the corner of the room. I pulled it alongside the bed and sat down.

I reached over and brushed her hair back from her face. A bruise spread along her left cheek just below her eye. I stroked her cheek with the back of my fingers. A single tear welled up in the corner of her eye, then broke and ran down her face.

"Honey, I'm so sorry about the baby . . ." I began.

More tears silently fell. "I told him. I told him I was pregnant. He just kept hitting me." Sam spoke with her eyes toward the ceiling.

"I told him I didn't know how to open the safe, but he didn't believe me. I begged him not to hit me anymore. He said he'd beat it out of me."

I listened as each word mixed inside me, and slowly turned to stone. A strange stone, a white-hot stone.

Sam turned to face me. "Leo, he said you'd stolen something from him. That's why he was there. He said if I gave it back to him, he'd let me live. Did you steal something, Leo?"

"No." I shook my head. "I've never stolen anything. What did he say I stole?"

"A key. I told him he was wrong. That he had the wrong person. That you wouldn't steal anything, but he just got angrier. He was sure it was in the safe. When I told him I couldn't open it, he just went crazy, hitting me. I was afraid he'd kill the baby, so I kicked him and tried to roll away. He was too strong. He pulled me back and said that if I didn't have sex

with him, he'd beat me so bad nothing would ever grow inside
of me."

I put my hand on her arm and squeezed her, timidly.

"So I did. He pulled down my pants and put himself inside
me. I don't remember much after that. I remember him holding
my arms down and grunting, then nothing. I went somewhere,
I don't know, way deep inside like it wasn't happening to me.
The next thing I remember was hearing your voice. I think he'd
just gone out the sliding glass door.

"So, I just missed him."

"Yes. I knew something was wrong with me, that he'd killed
the baby."

"Did you tell this to the police?"

"No. Not what he said about you. I wanted to hear it from
you before I told them anything."

"Tell me everything you can remember from the very begin-
ning. Can you do that? Maybe I can figure out who it was."

"Can I have some water first?"

I picked up her cup and tilted the straw into her mouth. She
took some small sips and then licked her lips.

"I had gone to Book 'N Card to pick up a couple of books
I'd ordered. When I came back, I parked the car, put the keys
in the front door, and this guy grabbed me from behind."

"Did you see his face?"

"No. Never. He grabbed my hair and told me not to look
around. He put a gun up to the side of my face and then hit
me with it to make his point." Sam touched her face and winced.

"Which hand had the gun?"

"His right."

"Can you remember his hand? Did you see it?"

"No. Just the barrel of the gun."

"Okay. Then what?"

"He pushed me into the house and back to the bedroom. He
had me put my hands behind my back and tied them up. Then
he put tape over my mouth."

"Did you see his hands then?"

Sam closed her eyes, then spoke. "Yes. They're white. Dirty. Short nails. He's white."

"Do you remember anything else? Rings, scars, tattoos, a smell to his hands?"

"Yes, they smelled. Gasoline, or motor oil, maybe."

"Any other smells? Sweat, body odor, cologne, tobacco?"

"His breath was terrible. Tobacco might have been part of it, also alcohol. I don't remember a cologne or anything."

"Good. Then what?"

"He pushed me down on the bed and tied something over my head. I was terrified then. I tried to kick him and he hit me in the head, with the gun, I think. He told me to lie still or he'd kill me. Then I felt something go around my neck and choke me. Some kind of noose."

"He used a sash and a belt of yours."

"He tied the noose to something because I couldn't move or I'd choke."

"Think back to when he grabbed you. Was he right behind you?"

"Yes."

"Where did his voice come from? Right in your ear? Up above you?"

"Above me. He was taller than me."

"Taller than me?" I asked.

"Maybe. At least as tall as you."

"His voice. Any accent? Southern, Boston, New York, Baltimore?"

"No. Nothing that sticks in my mind."

"Then what?"

"He left me there and went out and I heard him throwing things around and cursing."

"Was he alone? Did you hear any other voices?"

"No, only his. He must have been alone. When he came back to talk to me, all the crashing stopped. When he left, it started again."

I nodded and Sam went on. "I heard all kinds of noises. I

tried to get off the bed but I couldn't. Then he came back and asked me about the safe and started hitting me."

"Did he say anything more about this key I took?"

"No, just that you'd really fucked up this time and he was going to kill you. He started muttering 'Motherfucker' over and over like a chant."

"Then I came home."

"Yeah."

"You said he was too strong. How strong? Just stronger than you? Real strong? Stronger than me?"

Sam looked down at her arms. Finger bruises encircled her biceps. "Real strong, like you, weightlifter strong. I remember him holding my arms still."

The nurse stuck her head in the doorway. "Mr. Haggerty, you'll have to leave now. Visiting hours are over."

I waved her off. "Okay, just a couple of minutes.

"Sam, I have to go. I'll be back first thing in the morning. Honey, I feel so bad about what happened to you and losing the baby. I know how much you wanted one."

"Yeah," she said mournfully. "I felt so good. So ripe. I was already starting to nest. In my mind, you know. Fixing up a room for the baby, thinking about names. Now I'm just empty and I feel awful. Barren, that's the right word. Dead and ugly."

"I wish you'd told me, Sam."

"I wanted to, that night, but you didn't come home and I was hurt and angry."

"Mr. Haggerty."

"Okay. Sam, get some rest. I'll be back first thing in the morning."

"I'll try."

I stroked her arm, leaned over and kissed her featherlight on the cheek, right next to the bruise.

I passed the nurse on her way in with Sam's sedative on a tray. We exchanged brief conciliatory smiles.

In the lobby I called Arnie Kendall. A strange voice answered. "Hello."

"Arnie Kendall, please."

"Who's this?"

"Leo Haggerty. Who're you?"

There was no answer, then "Detective Lieutenant Arbaugh."

"I want to talk to Arnie." What kind of trouble was he in?

"Sorry, Mr. Haggerty. Phone won't reach that far."

"Why is that?" Mr. Smartass detective.

"Because he's dead."

9

"How'd it happen?" I asked, turning around in the phone booth to face the waiting room. I had left my gun in the car and felt paranoid and naked. Hospital manners, I guess.

"He was shot on the street. Looks like a drug buy went sour."

"Bullshit. You couldn't be more wrong. Arnie Kendall despised drugs."

"That's real interesting, Mr. Haggerty. Just how do you know Mr. Kendall?"

"We're friends and we've worked together."

"Is that so? You a bounty hunter, too?"

"No. I'm a private detective. I've backed him up a few times."

"Well, he sure had no backup this time."

"Tell you what, Lieutenant Arbaugh, I'm on my way home, why don't I swing by Arnie's place and you can tell me what you know and I'll tell you what I know. Maybe I can fill in some of the blanks."

"I've got a better idea, Mr. Haggerty. You give me your address and I'll come by your place. There's too many people underfoot here already."

"I thought you said he was shot on the street?"

"He was. After we identified the body, we called the home. When we got no answer, a patrol car came by and found his place had been trashed. So we've got a crime scene team crawling all over this mess."

I felt another turn on the vise my life had become.

"How about we split the difference. You know the Skyline Chili in Yorktown Shopping Center? I'll see you there in say five minutes."

"Ten."

"See you there."

I dropped another quarter in the slot and called Rocky Franklin.

Tawni, his fifth wife, answered the phone. All his wives had names that ended in "i," like Bambi, Toni, Vicki. Maybe his next two would be Dopi and Grumpi. She went to get Rocky.

"Yeah, Leo, what's up?"

"I need a bodyguard for Samantha, Rocky. A woman. A nurse-bodyguard, and I need her ten minutes ago."

"What happened?"

"She was attacked at home earlier today. They won't let me stay in the room, but a private-duty nurse can. I don't want her left alone. There's some kind of serious shit flying around me and I'm trying to get to the bottom of it."

"Consider it done. Hold on a second, I'll get someone lined up."

"Rocky, can you do it for me? I've got to get out of here, now."

"Sure, Leo. Whatever you need. I'm real sorry about Sam. Is she gonna be okay?"

"I think so, Rocky. I don't know when, but I think so."

"Where is she?"

I gave him the address and final instructions for the minder.

"I'll call in tomorrow and let you know what's happening. And thanks."

"Sure. I don't know what's happening, Leo, but stay frosty. You hear me?"

"Yeah, Rocky. I'm frosty."

I hung up the phone and ran to my car. Before starting the

engine, I took my Colt .45 out of the glove compartment and holstered it. From the hospital I made my way down Gallows Road, across Route 50 to the shopping center. I parked and crossed over to the Skyline Chili Parlor. It was pretty late so the place was empty. I ordered a cup of coffee and sat down. Five minutes later, a man entered the restaurant and stood peering at each table. I waved him over.

He stood over me and held out his badge. I read it.

"Have a seat, Lieutenant. Let's talk."

Arbaugh slid in and flipped open his notepad.

"First let me get your name, address, and phone numbers."

I recited the information and Arbaugh wrote it all down.

"Where were you earlier today, Mr. Haggerty?"

"When?"

"Just tell me about your day."

I ran through it quickly.

Arbaugh honed in on my activities between twelve and three. I told him Kelly and some of the investigators could verify that I was in my office all afternoon.

"Am I a suspect?"

"Not really, but the more people I can remove from the running, the easier my job is."

I sipped my coffee. Arbaugh motioned for a cup. He was one of those bald men who has a ridiculous swirl of hair from just above his ear that sits on top of his head like ice cream on a cone. It shrieked, "I'm bald and I hate it." Arbaugh fixed me with a professionally empty look.

"Tell me how Arnie died."

"Like I said, he was shot on the street."

"Fuck you, Arbaugh. I'm not a suspect. I'm trying to help. The man was a good friend of mine. You tell me what happened, maybe I can make some sense of it. I know his habits, his quirks. This isn't D.C., you know. I'd think that a homicide out here still has some novelty value at least."

Arbaugh reddened but said nothing. "He was shot in a parking lot about one p.m. Shotgun at close range."

"Why did you say it looked like a drug deal gone sour?"

"Hey, eight out of ten, that's what it is these days. But we found a tape on his answer machine. He got a call from a woman wanting to set up a meeting to discuss a job."

"What kind of job?"

"She said she'd bailed her boyfriend out and she was afraid he was going to bolt. Wanted her collateral protected."

"You got anything on this woman?"

"Oh yeah, we've got her body down at the morgue. Right next to Kendall's."

"How'd she buy it?"

"Looks like your friend walked over from his car to meet with this woman. . . ." Arbaugh's coffee arrived and he sipped it hesitantly. "Something caught his eye and he put a spring-loaded blade right through her throat. Damn near stapled her to the seat. Good thing he did. She had a .38 snubby in her lap. Probably was going to shoot him through the door."

"He probably saw it in her rear-view mirror when he approached the car. What'd she look like?"

"Standard issue bimbo. Bleached blond hair, lots of makeup, hot pants and a halter. Lots of tit showing."

"She was the bait."

"Well, your friend didn't bite, that's for sure."

"Who killed him, then?"

"We think there was somebody in the trunk. After nailing the girl, your friend fell backwards. At least that's what the angle of entry says he did, pulled his piece, and fired up at someone in the trunk."

"Did he hit him?"

"No bloodstains, but he could have been armored. Hell, everybody is these days."

"You said it was a shotgun. What kind?"

"Twelve-gauge, double-ought. First shot hit him in the chest falling backward. Kendall traded fire going down. We found three casings on the ground next to him. Second shot was to the head. The guy stood over him point blank and just blew it off." Arbaugh looked at me, waiting for a reaction.

I let him wait. "The car radio was on, loud. Right?"

"Yeah. It was way up. How'd you know that?"

"You'd do that to cover the sound of the trunk opening. Arnie heard that and knew what was happening. He fell back to cut down his exposure."

I imagined Arnie approaching the car. His eyes drawn to the cleavage, then checking the mirror. Seeing the gun. Adding up the too-loud radio. First the blade, then the gun. I could see it all. Right up to the shotgun blast. That wasn't right. It couldn't happen that way. Arnie was the most careful, most dangerous man I'd ever known. He was invincible. He would die at eighty, working in his ceremonial garden. Not like this.

"You okay? You look a little pale," Arbaugh asked.

"Yeah, yeah. I'm okay. What do you know about the girl?"

"Not much. Name was Renee Dubois. We're running her prints. See if she's on file anywhere."

"How about the car?"

"Nothing. Stolen. No prints but the girl's. Her partner must have been wearing gloves."

Arbaugh clicked his pen and said, "Does this sound like anybody you know?"

"No. It's a well-planned ambush. They knew enough about Arnie that he wouldn't be easy to get close to. But nobody comes to mind. It feels military, that's all I can say. Maybe somebody Arnie knew in 'Nam."

"Yeah, we saw the medals in his house. That's a thought. We'll follow up on it. How about more recent enemies? Anybody he put behind bars threaten to kill him?"

"Nobody that he mentioned. He had files of all his jobs. You can check to see if anybody's been released or escaped."

"We already are. What about angry family members?"

"Like I said, if there were any threats, he didn't mention them to me."

"Okay. If anything does come up, give me a call, any time

at all. He pissed somebody off big time, enough to get wasted for it. So there's a motive out there, a big one. Once we've got that we're halfway home." Arbaugh handed me his card.

"Yeah, if I think of anything, I'll call you."

"By the way, did he have any next of kin?"

"No. Arnie was raised in a bunch of foster homes. If he had any siblings, he didn't know about them. His mother died when he was fifteen. His father was an unknown white male. I'm the closest thing to his next of kin. Why?"

"We've got his car over on the impound lot. Would you mind getting it picked up? It'll just cost his estate for every day we have to store it."

His estate, right. "Sure, I'll get it taken care of tomorrow. What about his house? Can I go in and straighten the place up? I need to see if he's got a will on file. What he wanted in the way of burial. He's entitled to Arlington."

"Yeah, sure. We're done with the place." Arbaugh stood up. I rose and we shook hands.

I sat in the shop until I saw his car disappear. Then I left and drove home. I had a war to wage.

10

I ripped the yellow police banner from across the front door. Gift wrap for a disaster area. I stood there and looked at my house like it was a stranger's. Somebody had done me a real service, cutting me loose from my possessions. After Sam and Arnie, and a nameless child, this mess was like confetti. Once inside, I went into my office and found my microcassette recorder.

I started in the living room, analyzing the destruction as if it was a huge three-dimensional signature. I walked around speaking each question, each observation into the recorder.

First, must get to Snipes. Only common case we've had recently. What is connection to attacker? How did this guy find me? He'd already killed Arnie and trashed his place. Arnie told him nothing. My name on something on Arnie's place? A call to my office to see if I was in? Ask Kelly. Arnie: was the ambush an attempt to surprise and capture him? Why? Information? Just a hit? He knew Arnie was careful and quick. How? Why the second shot? Overkill? Angry? Frustrated?

I looked at the living room: the TV screen shattered, the CD and tape player destroyed, all the videotapes dumped, the art on the walls slashed, the glass shattered, the seating overturned and slashed.

He felt he had all day. No hurry. Knew when I'd come home? How? Maybe he was on drugs, didn't care if I came in? Not a pro, wasted time on pointless damage. Angry. No effort to hide search. Didn't care if I knew. Why? Thinks I stole something of his. Thinks I know who he is and he knows me. No mystery to keep secret. Why not come in alone? Why grab Sam?

I walked into the kitchen. There was food and broken china and glass all over the floor. The drawers were turned over and piled in a corner. Cupboards were open and everything in them had been swept onto the floor, or the counters.

Why did he hood Sam? So she couldn't identify him. He didn't want to kill her. A message to me? So there'd be no mistake about who did this? Why tell her about the key? He thinks I'm a thief. Key? Drugs? Therefore I won't go to the cops about this. Thinks it's going to be settled between us. How right you are, my friend.

I stepped over the books in the doorway into my office. He'd ripped off the shelves and dumped them on the floor. My word processor screen was shattered. Sam's manuscript was dumped on the floor, but he hadn't destroyed it. Illiterate bastard didn't know its worth. Small blessings. My files were all over the floor along with the contents of my desk. Only the floor safe and my gun case were untouched.

The bathroom had linens in the tub and toiletries in the sink. The toilet tank was uncovered. This guy works alone? Why? No friends? Can't trust anybody? Does his own work. No, not true. Had girl help him with Arnie. But does his own work. He's there on the scene, no hired stand-ins.

I pushed open the bedroom door and stood there. I started to gag at the bloodstain on the bed and walked back to the living room. Impulsive. Got angry about safe. Took time out to rape Sam, not finish his job. Didn't toss the bedroom. Likes surprise. Odds in his favor. Ambush on Arnie. Maybe waiting for me when Sam came home first? Not there long. Didn't see her leave for bookstore. Didn't want to face me. Wants to kill me. Thinks I stole a key of his. It'll be an ambush.

What did Sam say? Right-handed, white, no accent. Breath—tobacco and alcohol. Gasoline or oil on hands. Tall as me, strong as me.

I clicked off my recorder and went back to the bedroom. I pulled down a suitcase and tossed some clothes into it. If I needed anything else, I'd buy it. I walked over to the bathroom, came back with a few toiletries, and tossed them in. Zipping up the bag, I carried it to my office. A checkbook and personal phonebook went into one pocket.

I unlocked the gun case and pulled out a box of .45-caliber hydroshock slugs, and tossed them into the other pocket.

Under a mound of papers and books I found the picture of Sam that had stood on my desk. The glass was cracked but the picture was unharmed. I slipped it from the frame and stared at it.

Sam, sleek and brown, was standing in the clear blue water on a clean white beach. She had a quizzical look on her face, almost a squint. Later I asked her if it was the sun. She said no. She had realized that she was happier than she'd ever been before and she was wondering when it would end.

I memorized her features. The thick chestnut hair framing her face. Her widow's peak. Her bright green eyes, so often mischievous. The deep dimpled smile, generous and easy. With that in my suitcase, I picked it up, turned off the lights, and left the house.

11

The Bed-a-Bye Motel had all the comforts I sought. A firm
bed, a working air conditioner and phone, and no obvious
spores, molds, or fungi. I registered as Barney Rubble and paid
cash.

Once in the room, I set my bag on the dresser, sat down on
the bed, and called a friend.

"Speak," a bass voice growled.

"Wardell, it's Leo Haggerty. Is the Rev there?"

No answer. I guess he was checking.

"Leo, what's happening, baby?" the Rev sang into my ear.

"Too much, Rev. I got trouble enough for you and me. I
need some help."

"Talk to me, buddy." The Rev is Reverend Schafrath Brown,
minister of the Church of Divine Intervention and Street Jus-
tice. He and his sidekick, Wardell Blevins, also do some part-
time bounty hunting. Arnie and I had worked with and against
them before.

"There's a guy hunting me. He's already killed Arnie . . ."

"Shit, man, I'm sorry to hear that. Who'd you piss off, the
Terminator?"

"I'll let you know when I find him. Right now, I'm lying low, but I need somebody protected. I don't want this bastard getting ahold of anyone close to me and hurting them."

"You want Sam covered?"

"No. I've got somebody on her. It's a girl, Randi Benson. She's a student at Bolton Farms School. I'm her legal guardian. I'm going to call her right now and describe you and Wardell to her. Go to the dormitory called Forsythe Hall and call up for her. She's in Room 16. When you get her, lose yourselves."

"For how long?"

"Until this is done. I'll call my answering service every day and leave a message. Check for it at midnight. No message for three days, assume I'm dead. When it's all over, I'll come in person to the church and I'll wait there until you show up. Bring the girl to the church. Don't turn her over to anyone but me. Got it?"

"Done, buddy."

"Thanks. How's my credit these days?"

"No problem. We'll square this when it's over."

"Thanks, Rev. One last thing. Three days and no message, call my attorney, Walter O'Neil. He has my will. He knows who gets what. Okay?"

"All right. Good luck, man."

"Thanks. I'll need it."

Three rings later and I heard Randi's sleepy voice mumble "Hello?"

"Randi, it's Leo. I'm in a lot of trouble and you may be too, so pay attention."

"What's the matter?" Apprehension cut through her fog.

"Somebody's trying to kill me and I'm afraid they may go after you to use as leverage against me. I'm sending two men out to guard you. They'll be there in about forty-five minutes. Go pack some things for yourself and wait for them. When they come to the dorm, they'll call up for you. Go down with another girl. If it's not the two guys I describe . . ."

"Isn't Arnie one of them? I know what he looks like."

"No, honey, Arnie won't be one of them. Arnie's dead. Whoever killed him is looking for me."

"Oh God. Who did it?"

"I don't know yet. We don't have time to talk. Just listen and do as I say."

"Okay."

"The two men are Schafrath Brown and Wardell Blevins. Brown is short, five feet five or so, dapper, bald head, pencil-thin mustache. Wardell's a beast, six feet eight, three hundred pounds. Has one of those Whoopi Goldberg hairdos, looks like a tarantula on his head. He cracks his knuckles constantly, drive you crazy.

"You can trust them. They'll protect you until it's all over and you're safe. Then they'll bring you to me. If it isn't them, go upstairs, lock your door, and call the police. Use 911. Then call me on my beeper. Do you remember the number?"

"Yes. Why can't I be with you, Leo?"

"Because I'm the target, honey. I'm the last person you want to be around."

"How about somewhere with Sam?"

"Randi, the guy who's after me attacked Sam today at the house . . ."

"Oh no, is she okay?"

"Yeah, she's okay. She's alive. She's at the hospital and I left her with a bodyguard. I have to disappear for a while and try to find out who's after me and why. Now go do what I said, and Randi . . ."

"Yes."

"Don't tell anyone, I mean *anyone*, that you're going any-where or with whom. You want to disappear, understand?"

"Yes. I'm scared, Leo."

"I know. These guys'll protect you. You'll be okay. Now go."

"Leo."

"Yes."

"Please be careful. I love you."

"I will and I love you too. Now scoot."

I lay back on the bed and laced my fingers behind my head. I had a slight head start on Arbaugh and Rhodasson. Neither one struck me as a dummy. They'd start cross-checking names and places pretty soon and be back looking for me. Sam, holding back what the man had said to her, gave me another half-step lead. If it was going to keep me alive to meet him, I'd better be on the job early tomorrow.

I pulled out my address book, flipped to the blank pages in the back, and made notes for the next day. A shower did nothing for me. Stripped to my shorts, I reloaded my Colt with the hydroshock shells. Hollowpoints, guaranteed to expand to .90 caliber on impact. I dropped a couple of slugs and found my hands trembling again. Fear, rage, anticipation? All three, I guessed. My mind was filled with the faceless man. I could focus on him. Any thought of Sam in the hospital and my mind fled. I saw her but felt little.

Didn't I love her? Why was I so empty now? Maybe this was one of those changes that Dr. Berger had promised me. I tried visualizing Arnie. I could see him. I could say he was dead, but I didn't believe it. Nothing there. I'm a stone all right, all the way through. I stood up and walked aimlessly across the room a couple of times. When I sat down, I pulled out the Colt and reloaded it. I sat and fiddled with it for a while. Stay frosty, stay empty. I had things to do.

In bed, I lay there staring at the dark ceiling, unable to sleep. I had no thoughts, just a crackling energy that I couldn't dissipate.

12

I spent the night tossing and turning, like I was sleeping on a spit. At seven I gave myself permission to stop trying to sleep and move on to showering.

By eight I was sitting in my car on I-95 sipping lukewarm rehydrated carcinogens and wondering how commuters endured "The Crawl" twice a day. To find affordable housing near D.C. now meant living in your car for four hours each day.

Thirty minutes later, I crossed over the Potomac and rolled past a graffiti-enhanced sign that read "Welcome to Washington, A District of Colombia." Amen to that. I'd been born and raised in D.C. But these days it was no place to live. The drug wars had made it Murder City, the most lethal place in America two years running. The police chief had announced that the killings would stop when the turf wars were settled. That was a comforting bit of news. The city's hospitals couldn't treat their cardiac patients because the operating rooms were full of gunshot victims. There was a growing backup in autopsies because the medical examiner's office couldn't keep up with the deluge of the dead. All that medical work, and the city schools had to cancel some athletic events because they couldn't provide trainers for the games. It's easier to shoot bullets than baskets in the capital city.

I called my secretary.

"Franklin Investigations. How may I help you?"

"Kelly, it's Leo. I'm not coming in today. Transfer any calls to Stuart, okay. If it's an absolute emergency, you call me on my beeper, and I'll decide who should handle it."

"Okay, Leo."

"I want you to do something for me. Call the Fairfax County Morgue. Find out if they've finished the autopsy on Arnie Kendall. If so, see if the death certificate has been filed. When that's done, have somebody from the office go down and sign a release for the body and get his personal effects. Call a local funeral home, have them pick up the body, cremate it, and keep the remains until I can pick them up. Send someone by with a check from the office."

"Do you want me to phone in an obituary, Leo?"

"No."

"Will there be a service?"

"No. No service."

After a brief silence Kelly said, "Okay."

"One last thing. Were there any calls for me yesterday, just asking if I was in or what my schedule was?"

"No. None that I can recall. I gave you all your messages yesterday."

"Maybe this caller didn't leave a message or a name. Just wanted to know if I was in."

"No. I always ask for a name. If they wouldn't give me one, I'd remember that. There weren't any calls like that."

"Okay. Thanks, Kelly. I'll be checking in later on."

"All right, Leo."

I called Sam's room and got no answer. Damn, what if she was going in for the D&C right now? Shit. I thought about turning around and going to the hospital. No. I wasn't going anywhere near her or anyone else I cared about. I was shit drawing flies. My best chance of staying alive was staying away from places this guy already knew about.

If I wanted to stay a step ahead of Arbaugh and Rhodasson, and I dearly wanted that, I had to make my move now.

I pulled into the visitors' lot at the station house, parked, and trotted up the front steps. Inside, I signed in, went through the metal detector, and turned in my gun. Outside the interview rooms I told the officer on duty who I wanted to talk to and why. I was photographed and my identification was checked. He let me into interview room 3 and told me to wait.

I took a seat with my back to the door and did as I was told. Behind me, the door opened and closed. I didn't stand up. The man I wanted to talk to came around the table and held out his hand.

I took his hand from the outside, twisted it over, and bent it back. Smiling, I looked up into his startled face.

"Hello, Harold. Nice to see you again."

"Jesus Christ, let go of my hand. You're breaking it."

"Sit down, Harold, and look glad to see me or you'll jerk off with your left hand from now on."

Harold tried to smile while I kept the pressure on.

"Real simple now, Harold, tell me what you stole and from whom?"

"I don't know what you're talking about," he whimpered.

"Too bad." One quick twist and Harold groaned and rose up on his toes.

"Here goes the whole arm, Harold. Say goodbye."

"All I gotta do is holler and they'll throw your ass out of here."

"That's right, but the first thing I'm going to do when I leave here is belt a cop and get myself thrown in here with you. See, I'm under a death sentence out there, Harold. And you put it on me. So, if I'm going, I'm taking you with me. First exercise break, Harold, and you're mine. Once more, Harold. What did you take and from whom?"

"All right, all right. I was looking to split town. I was out on bond, but no way was I gonna stand trial. So I was at this party with Bonnie."

"Who's Bonnie?"

"My old lady. The one your friend busted up when you came to get me."

"Okay. Go on."

"Well, there was a party going on. I was trying to get some dough together so I could skip town. Anyway, I didn't get a hell of a lot. Not enough to go very far on. So I was hanging out, drinking, and this one guy, he's bragging that he'd ripped off something big. So I hung around and watched. He kept patting his pants when he talked about it. He got pretty ripped and shacked up with Renee. When he was out, I slipped in and went through his pants. I figured I wouldn't get caught."

Well, we all knew how that turned out. "Then what?"

"Renee must have seen me sneak in. She told him who I was. Next thing I know he's in here visiting me. You know the rest."

"Yeah, but tell me anyway."

"I told him you guys ripped me off. That you were bounty hunters from the bonding company and when you were searching me you found the key . . ."

"What key? You didn't have any drugs on you."

"No, a key. You know, to a locker. So I told him the bonding company's name. Figured he could take it from there."

Harold chewed on a thumbnail.

"Harold, we're not done yet. Where's the key?"

"I stuffed it in the back seat of the car when I was getting out at the station. I had to roll over on my belly so I could slide out. That's when I did it."

"Why didn't you keep it with you?"

"I didn't want to give it to the property people. They might have gotten curious and figured out what the key was for. I didn't need to get tied to any more trouble. Or they might have ripped it off. That happens all the time down here."

"Really? That's awful. Well, we're almost done here, Harold. What's the guy's name?"

"I don't know. I never met him before."

"Give me a description."

"About your size. Real strong. Skin's real tan, looks like leather. He's a skinhead. Has a mustache and a beard thing. I don't know what you call it."

"A van dyke?"

"Yeah, that's it. He doesn't have any lips. I mean, not really. It's just his mouth looks like a fucking scar. It's weird."

"Anything else?"

"No."

"What about his work?"

"I don't know."

"Who's Renee?"

"Just a cunt. It was her party. She dances with Bonnie."

"Where?"

"The Diamond Slipper on Georgia Avenue."

"She know this guy?"

"I don't know. I don't think so. She was hitting on him. The way they were talking, I don't think she knew him before."

I let go of Harold's hand and leaned back. There was something all wrong about this, but I didn't know what. I ran through his story again, trying to get his actions to lie down with his motives. There were two things that just didn't make sense. I played with them until I came to a new appreciation of Harold.

"Why such a nice guy, Harold? First, you tell this guy exactly what he wants to know, and now you tell me what I want. I don't see a merit badge in this for you, Harold."

"What's your problem? I gave you what you wanted. Isn't that good enough?"

"That's it. It's too good. So I don't trust it. Even in here you need money, Harold. For a lawyer, for starters. Bonnie could have gotten that key for you. Unless you aren't going to be in here." I let that thought blossom.

"Oh Harold, you rodent, you. You're going to roll over on

your buddies. Then into the Witness Protection Program. You don't need money. They'll get you a job, a new Bonnie, a new everything. So you sicced that fucker on us."

Harold pulled his lips back over his tusks and let his head bob in silent glee. "You guys fucked me over, bringing me in. Just thought I'd return the favor."

"And you gave me what I wanted, so I wouldn't come in here and fuck it all up for you."

"That's right, Jew-lover. Now you gotta go looking for him. And hope you find him before he finds you."

"You told him Arnie was the tough nut. No talking to him. He should whack him right off, then go to work on me."

Harold sniggered. "Guess I was right, wasn't I? You're the one here all bent out of shape."

"Enjoy it while you can, Harold. If that key isn't in the car, I'm going to have to come back and talk to you again. Fatally."

13

The guy must have been pretty desperate to come into the police station after Harold. I know I was. Maybe he left some useful information when he signed in. A look at the photo they took of him would help quite a bit. As I walked back to the check-in station, I tried to compose a story that would get me what I wanted. I'd signed in using my real name and told them that I was the investigator hired by Harold's attorney and needed to talk to the client about what happened. I got my story straight and was prepared to use it, when I saw Rhodasson and Arbaugh walking down the hall. They had their heads together and were pointing at something in a file Rhodasson carried. I turned toward the wall and studied wanted posters and personnel notices. Walk on by, I urged them silently. I saw my scant lead over them shrinking to nothing. Where were the moron cops of TV when you needed them.

Rhodasson and Arbaugh were at the check-in desk asking to see the visitor list. That was my cue to leave. I turned away from them, ambled across the hall, and right out the front door.

I left the parking lot as unobtrusively as possible. I couldn't move this guy from Renee's party to the jail without going through Bonnie. Who else knew where Harold had gone?

On my way to Bonnie's house I called the office.

"Kelly, Leo here. Couple more things for you. First call Bolton Farms School. Ask for the seniors' guidance counselor and tell her that Randi Benson will be out of school for the rest of the week. Sudden death in the family." I thought of where the Rev would hide her. He hated cold weather. So did Wardell. "She's back in North Dakota for the services and so on. Tell her I picked her up very late last night. Explain that you're calling for me, I'm her legal guardian, and if necessary I'll call her later to confirm it. Got that?"

"Uh-huh. What's next?"

"Who went to the morgue to get Arnie's personal effects?"

"Bobby Lee. He's going from there to the Parson's Funeral Home to arrange for the cremation."

"Fine. Call Bobby and have him go from the funeral home to the D.C. police impound yard. Tell him to go through Arnie's car. The keys should be in his effects. Tell him to feel back behind the rear-seat cushion for a key, a locker key. When he's got it, have him call me on my car phone or my beeper. I'll get right back to him. Tell him to assume he's being tailed and I'll give him instructions to meet me once he's on the road."

"Okay. I'll get right on it."

Kelly was the first person I hired when I took over. Her predecessor typed twenty-five errors per minute and thought taking dictation was something you did on your knees. She must have thought she was working on Capitol Hill. I hired Kelly right out of high school. She'd been in the Voc. Ed. track even though she was clearly bright enough for academic work. A string of foster home placements had put a big dent in her self-confidence. Two years with us and she was starting to take courses at NOVA with an eye to a criminology degree from George Mason.

Bonnie's house was a half-hour drive. I pulled up in front and parked. Four days ago this place had been a fortress to be stormed. Now it was a rundown duplex with a patchy crabgrass lawn and peeling siding.

I stepped out of the car and glanced up and down the street. No cars with occupants. I tried to convince myself that he wouldn't be here. He'd already gotten what he wanted, the next link in the chain to his precious key. No reason to return here. No reason at all. I shrugged a little so my holster felt more accessible and walked across the yard to the front steps.

I pulled back the screen and rapped on the door. No answer. I rapped again. The other door flew open and a figure jumped out onto the divided porch. I whipped out my .45 and nearly blew a hole through a ten-year-old boy who hollered, "See you later, Mom," and scampered down the steps and out to the street.

I holstered my gun, took a deep breath, and exhaled slowly through pursed lips. Get a grip, Haggerty. I was shaken. Not just by what I'd almost done but by how thin my veneer of competence was.

I rapped a third time on the door, then tried the handle. Unlocked. After the unpleasant visitors she'd been having lately, I thought Bonnie'd use more care. I pushed open the door and called her name. Then again.

Out came my pistol and I stepped into the house. It was surprisingly cold. The thermostat read 55. An ugly thought started to form. The living room bore his stamp, neo-modern chaos. A quick peek into the kitchen showed more of the same. The bathroom was empty.

I approached the stairs and went up with a sideways cross-step like a cantering horse. My gun swung in a constant arc. My head passed the level of the upper floor and I saw that the bedroom doors were open. A window air conditioner labored and whined. First, the bathroom. I pushed open the door. It was empty.

Something floated in the tub. I stepped closer and saw an archipelago in the murky water. Toes, a knee, the navel island, two nipples, and her nose. Bonnie floated mutely, her eyes wide open. A cord around her neck anchored her to the drain.

I put my finger in the tub. Still cold. That and the chill air and it would be a while before anyone knew she was here. Wreak havoc with the time of death, too.

Arbaugh and Rhodasson would be on their way over here pretty soon. I'd already left a memorable impression on the front porch if anyone was watching.

I decided not to search the place but just scan what was already exposed. Nothing in the front bedroom. The middle room was full of Harold's Nazi paraphernalia, including posters, flags, helmets, insignia, and a ton of propaganda. I grabbed a few copies of the Fourth Reich's newsletter *Call to Arms* and headed for the door.

Driving back to Virginia, I called Sam's room and got no answer.

Ten minutes later my phone rang.

"Leo, Bobby Lee. I got your key."

"What kind is it?"

"Storage locker. Number on it is 312."

"Anything else?"

"Nope."

"Is the company name on the key? The company that manufactured it."

"Yeah, Amerilock Corporation."

"Okay. Does it have a plastic cover on the top?"

"Yeah, bright red."

"Okay. Call Amerilock. Tell them you have a locker key, the number, and the cover color. That's how they code the location for the keys they sell to storage companies. When they tell you where the locker is located, go down and empty it. Take Clancy with you. The guy who wants that key has already killed twice for it. Assume you're being tailed. Once you've got what's in the locker, call me on my beeper and we'll arrange for a transfer."

"On my way."

14

I called the hospital again. This time there was an answer. The nurse who took the call put me on hold while she got her supervisor.

"Hello," she said.

"Yes, this is Leo Haggerty. Is my wife there?"

"What's your wife's name?"

"Clayton, Samantha Clayton."

"I'm sorry, Mr. Haggerty, but your wife checked out a little while ago."

"Didn't she have a D&C scheduled for this afternoon?"

"Yes, but there was a change in the operating-room schedules, so she was moved up and had the procedure this morning. We advised her to stay overnight but she refused and discharged herself."

Shit. "The private-duty nurse she had, did that person go with her?"

"I don't know, Mr. Haggerty, but I believe so."

At least something hadn't gone wrong. "How long ago did she leave?"

"About forty-five minutes."

"Thank you."

I hung up, called Kelly, and asked if Sam had called the office.

"No. But the nurse you hired, Mrs. Sorenson, did."

"Was there a message?"

"No. But she left a number and asked you to call right away."

"Okay, give it to me."

She read it off and I wrote it down. "Any other calls?"

"Clancy called. He's with Bobby. He said they were on their way to a storage locker to get something for you. He said he'd call you directly when he actually had it."

"Thanks."

I hung up and dialed Mrs. Sorenson. She picked up on the fourth ring.

"Hello."

"Mrs. Sorenson, this is Leo Haggerty. You were contacted by Rocky Franklin to watch my wife, Samantha. I understand she left the hospital. Is she there with you?"

"No, Mr. Haggerty, she's not."

"Do you know where she is?"

"First, Mr. Haggerty, I need to confirm your identity. The scars on your left leg, how did you get them?"

At least Rocky was thinking. "I tore my knee up playing lacrosse. Torn cartilage and a dislocated kneecap. The surgery was to fix the damage. The surgeon was Geoff Whitney. He did it in 1973. It was pre-arthroscopy, so they look like railroad tracks. Do you want any more?"

"That's sufficient, Mr. Haggerty. Your wife signed herself out against the doctor's advice. I believe she was distressed by your absence and did not want to wait for you or be in the hospital anymore."

"Where did she go?"

"She went to your home. She packed a small bag and left in the cab we took from the hospital."

"Why didn't you stay with her?"

"She fired me, Mr. Haggerty. She said she didn't want any

protection and that if I attempted to stop her or to follow her she'd report me to the police."

"Great. Did she say anything else?"

"No. Nothing at all. However, watching her pack, I'd say she was pretty angry. She was throwing things around and kicking things out of her way when she left."

"Were you followed from the hospital?"

"No. I checked on that."

"How about when the cab left the house?"

"Nobody followed it."

"Okay. Thanks for your help. Send your bill to my office."

"There's one last thing, Mr. Haggerty."

"Yes?"

"The cab was a Universal, Number 31. He left here at 2:38."

"Good thinking."

While I was concocting a story for the Universal dispatcher, my beeper went off. I checked the number of the call and dialed it.

"Hello."

"Clancy, it's Leo, what have you got?"

"It's a data disk, Leo. For a computer."

"Any markings on it?"

"None."

"All right. Let's make the exchange at Tysons Corner."

"One or Two?"

"One. You know the escalators near the middle, about half-way between Hecht's and Bloomingdale's?"

"Yeah."

"Okay, you park on the upper level, then hang around the escalator until you see me at the bottom. When I go up, you come down. Leave Bobby behind to watch your back."

"All right. When will you be there?"

I checked my watch. "Give me a half hour or so. If I'm not there by four, leave and I'll set it up again."

"See you there."

I dialed information, then Universal Cab Company.

"Universal Cab. May I help you?"

"Yes, this is Dr. Kenworthy, Valleyview Mental Hospital. May I speak with your supervisor, please?"

"Hold one minute." While I held, I mused on the pastoral motif in naming mental-health facilities. The healing power of chipmunks, mountain streams, and unmowed grass.

"This is Darnita Terry."

"This is Dr. Kenworthy. One of our patients, Samantha Clayton, was picked up today by your cab Number 31, a little after two-thirty p.m. She was supposed to be dropped at our aftercare facility on Rolling Road. Well, she hasn't shown up there and it's quite late. Ms. Clayton is just out of the hospital for her latest suicide attempt and we're quite concerned. She's due for her Stelazine before five p.m. Can you contact this cab? If he's broken down en route we'll send someone to get her."

"Let me call that unit and I'll get right back to you, Doctor."

"I'd rather hold on and wait, if that's okay."

"Of course." She clicked off and I drummed my hand on the steering wheel.

A minute later she was back. "Dr. Kenworthy, our driver dropped your patient off about forty-five minutes ago."

"That's not possible. She never checked in at the center. Where was she dropped off? This is quite alarming, considering her history. She may be planning another attempt. She can be very cunning." I measured out the words for effect. "She may have lied to your driver about where she was to be dropped off. Can you get the address he left her off at? It's a start. I hope it wasn't just a street corner?"

"Hold on, Doctor. I'll radio the driver, see if I can get you an exact address."

"Thank you." I inflated the words with sincerity.

A minute later she told me it was Sandy Abrams's address. She was a friend of Sam's. I thanked her again, sang her praises, and headed toward Tysons Corner.

On my way over, I called Sandy and spoke to her machine.

"Sandy, it's Leo Haggerty. I'm trying to get in touch with Sam. I know she went to your place. Tell her she can reach me at any time on my beeper." I waited a second, then went on, "Sam, if you're there and you're listening to this, pick it up or call me. I'm in the car. We need to talk." I held on for thirty seconds, hoping she would cut off the tape and talk to me. When she didn't, I cradled the receiver in defeat.

Tysons Corner is a suburban satellite for Washington, D.C. It provides easy access to the halls of power in Washington, without the combat-zone ambience of the city. Corporate America isn't crazy about doing its business in Dodge City, and has moved out here. It's now one of the largest commercial centers in America. Fairfax County is still trying to convince itself that it isn't a city, just an ill-constructed intersection. The place needs its own government, not more turn lanes.

The land around here is too valuable to let people live on. Developers came in, bought up the next street over from mine, and leveled all the houses so they could put up an office building. It's not too bad, I guess. You take the money and run to Loudoun or Stafford and buy a farm with twenty or thirty acres.

With all that wealth clotting in one place, you have to find ways to dispose of it, and so there's more shopping than Imelda has shoes. Jerusalem for the Yuppite Kingdom. Every possible luxury for sale. A boutique devoted to every conceivable specialty. All things portable, white, or left-handed. Only musicboxes, a gadgeteria, designer cookies. Custom made, handmade, imported.

I pulled into the parking lot behind Nordstrom's, got out, walked through the store, and strolled down to Woodies. Inside Woodies, I took the escalator down to the lower level and walked toward Hecht's. When they'd expanded the mall, they put in an atrium roof and planted palm trees everywhere. In the distance, I could make out Bloomingdale's. Halfway there was a pair of escalators. I loitered near the bottom until I saw Clancy leaning against the railing above me. When our eyes met, we each moved to step onto the moving stairs. I scanned the people behind Clancy: a McLean matron on her way to or from Anne Klein, three giggling teenage girls, and an impeccably dressed black man, probably a salesman at Britches.

Clancy was doing the same for me. As we approached, he reached into his coat and pulled out the disk. When we passed, he slipped it into my palm and I dropped it into my inside jacket pocket. Nobody on his side even blinked. If anything was going on behind me, I trusted Clancy to take care of it. The rest of the ride was pleasantly dull.

When I stepped off the stairs, I saw Bobby Lee sitting on a bench eating a danish. He looked right through me. That meant no one had been loitering around the escalator while I was coming up. I walked past him and moved briskly to my car. Bobby would watch to see if anyone was following me and then fall in behind. I resisted the urge to break into a trot, to whistle, or suddenly spin around, and finally climbed into my car.

I turned on the engine, pulled out of my space, and meandered around the herd of cars to Route 7. Once on 7, I turned on the radio. Gene Ryder, local boy making good, was telling me that when he picks up his guitar, "It feels like a gun, feels like a gun, feels like a gun." Why doesn't it work the other way around?

15

Reed Carter Lewis V lives in Skyline City, a group of high-rise condominiums with their own mall and office buildings. It's quite possible to live an entire life within its walls, going from home to work and play through its tunnels and elevators. Reed leaves now and then, but most of the time he's home, so I didn't bother to call ahead.

I rode up to the twenty-fifth floor, got off, and walked down to his place. A couple of raps on the door and I heard someone move inside. I stepped back so he could get a better look through the peephole in his door. The door opened and Reed stood there smiling, arms out in greeting.

"Leo, nice to see you. What brings you here?"

"Trouble, Reed. That and your know-how."

"Come on in, come on in."

I followed Reed into his living-room office. He's an independent consultant for a number of local computer firms. He writes programs to solve problems or he solves problems in other people's programs. Either way he gets to work out of his home a lot, the hours that he wants, and like now, in his shorts and Tori Welles T-shirt. He shakes his head when he realizes how much money people pay him to do what he does and how he lives. It's a far cry from his childhood dreams as the fifth-generation son of the Lewises of Richmond. There had been a Lewis leading troops at Bull Run, and a Lewis on Teddy Roosevelt's flank. His grandfather was wounded at Châlons-sur-Marne and his father punched holes in the Germans for Patton. Everyone knew he'd come to a bad end when he refused to go to VMI and chose the Air Force Academy. Lewises had always been in the Army. Nothing else was acceptable. Somehow, high in the skies over Vietnam, perhaps it was the thin air, Reed began to question the family tradition of military service. Oh, dropping bombs on water buffalo from twenty-two thousand feet wasn't "the horror." It was the two Vietnamese girls he lived with and all the free time and rum with which he had to reflect upon things that eroded the "glorious nobility" of our cause and led him to reconsider pulling a full twenty in the cockpit of a B-52.

We'd met as neighbors and stayed friends ever since. I followed him through the foyer to the living room. He sat down in a swivel chair and held out his hand.

"So what do you have for me?"

I pulled out the disk and handed it to him. He looked at both sides, then handed it back.

"It's a computer disk, Leo, stores information."

"Heh, heh, Reed. I know I'm low-tech . . ."

"Low-tech, Leo? You're cyberphobic. You react to machinery like Dracula seeing the cross."

"Maybe. I'm getting better. I've got a car phone now."

Reed rocked back in the chair and clutched his chest.

"Oh no, not that, anything but that . . ." Then he spun around, reached under his desk, and came up with a black leather case.

"Okay, Leo, maybe you're ready for this baby." He put the case on his lap and popped it open. "New briefcase computer, with modem and fax machine, all in one. An entire office in your lap."

I threw my arm up in front of my face, cowered, and begged, "Put that away. It's killing me."

"Okay. What do you want to know about this baby?"

"Everything. Whose it is. What's on it. It's a very hot piece of merchandise, Reed. Two dead, already."

Reed flipped it back to me. "Shit, get that thing out of here."

"Relax. There's at least three layers between you and whoever is so hot to get it back. I wouldn't have come up here if I didn't think the transfer was clean." I flipped him the disk.

"You're sure?"

I nodded.

"Okay. Make yourself comfortable, this could take a while."

Reed spun in his chair, loaded the disk into his computer, and started checking it out. I walked around the living room. The long wall was floor-to-ceiling data disks, operating manuals, and texts. The rear wall was devoted to military history and biographies. Photographs of five generations of Lewis men were strategically placed amongst the books. I looked at the picture of the first Reed Lewis, a company commander for Stonewall Jackson. Reed may have rejected the family path for himself, but he still revered it in his family.

I always thought that a family that couldn't come up with another name for its eldest sons in one hundred years was a little short on imagination. Looking at number one's picture, I reconsidered. Genetics may have played a bigger part than I thought. It was the same exact face as his great-great-grandson's. The features were as thin, precise, and symmetrical as a geometry problem. The old photograph made it hard to judge flesh tones, but my friend couldn't keep a tan for ten minutes. Straight from pale to peel, like a shrimp. The thick wavy hair was red. I looked up at his son's picture. The only thing different was the shade of red. I checked the next two generations. Styles changed, shades varied, but the hair was always red. The eyes were always green. They were right. It would have been silly to give them different names.

I didn't even bother to look for a novel. In all the time I'd known him, I'd never seen Reed dally with fiction. I'd argued that making everything up might yield a different truth than recreating a life long over, but he wasn't having any of it.

"Anything to drink?" I asked.

"Yeah. I don't know what. Check the fridge."

V-8, grapefruit, and apricot juice were it. I poured a glass of V-8, sat in the dining nook, and turned on the TV. I was stunned by a majestically stupid movie about a cop named Brutus who among other activities of daily living dug bullets out of his body with his bare hands.

I knew I was in real trouble because the soundtrack was louder than the dialogue. Soundtrack volume is inversely related to the intelligence of the screenplay. At this level the writer must have been a chimpanzee.

When Brutus, shot in the shoulder, used that arm to pull up a man who was hanging from the roof of the building, I quit.

I started to dial the office, realized it was closed, and called Kelly at home.

"Hello?"

"Kelly, Leo. I'm sorry to call you at home, but I need something done first thing in the morning. It's important. The locker Clancy opened, get the number and location and call the rental company. Tell them you have a problem with the invoice for the rental charges. Dates, something. Have them confirm how long it was rented and to whom. Call me on my beeper when you get the name."

"Sure. Oh, by the way, there were a couple of calls for you before I left the office."

"Who was it?"

"Two policemen. One was named Arbaugh, the other Rhodasson. They wanted to talk to you."

"What did you tell them?"

"That you hadn't been in the office. That I didn't know where you were, but that if you did call in, I'd pass the message on."

"Okay, thanks. They may come by to visit if I don't get in touch with them soon. Don't let them bully you. You don't have to answer any of their questions. Just refer them to Rocky."

"Okay. Are you in some kind of trouble?"

"Nah. Nothing to worry about. Just a big misunderstanding. Couple of days, it'll be all straightened out. You just keep doing your job, that's all you need to be concerned with."

"Okay. I'll get on this first thing."

"Good. Talk to you tomorrow."

I walked across the room and looked over Reed's shoulder. "So what is it?"

"Well, there's two types of files here. The first looks like input files. The second is report files. Whoever ran the reports deleted the title which would tell us what the report is all about.

"Since these files are on the same disk, I would assume the input files were used by some type of program to generate these reports. That still doesn't tell us what the numbers mean. See there's one hundred and twenty entries for subjects here. Then they've got I.D. numbers. God knows what they are."

I looked at the row of numbers. "Social Security numbers. That's what they are. So the data sources are people. Then what?"

"Okay. Across the top are all these abbreviations. Then there's all these numbers entered for each heading. It's a data pool. The second file is the same subjects, same headings, different entries. I don't know how they're related. There are a number of these pairs of files, with different dates on them. Looks like the data gets entered at two different times. The first file is entered on Fridays, each week. Then the second pair is entered on the weekend. Same pattern for all the pairs, over a three-week period."

"What will you try to figure out first?"

"First, whether these columns are statistically related. Then I'll know which columns are means, standard deviations, and so on. Derivatives of the original raw data. It still won't tell us what the columns refer to, just that they are a coherent treatment of the data and how they're related. Then I'll see if one file is related to the other and how. That's about all I can do for you. You've got to find out whose data this is. There's nothing on the disk that identifies the owner of this stuff."

"How long will all this take?"

"Hard to say. Once I figure out the source codes, it may all unravel pretty quickly, but that could take quite a while."

"Can you give this a priority?"

"Hey, what are friends for. Besides, I like the challenge."

"Thanks, Reed. Keep crunching it. Call me as soon as you get anything out of this stuff. Here's my beeper number. Call me day or night. One other thing."

"Yeah?"

"Don't mention this to anyone. Nobody knows you've got this disk. Let's keep it that way."

"My sentiments exactly."

I waved to him and said, "I'll let myself out." He turned back to the black screen and reached for another disk.

16

The Bed-a-Bye Motel was just where I left it. I repossessed room Number 14 without fanfare and sat at the Formica desk. I was too damned tired to write my notes on the pad I had left there. I tried to recall dinner but drew a blank. Dial-a-Pizza was an option, but even that felt too difficult. I lay down on the bed, pulled the phone over next to me, and tucked it under my arm like an old friend.

Sandy Abrams's machine was on. I waited through the message, then spoke. "Sandy or Sam, this is Leo. I need to talk to you. Please call my beeper. The number is . . ."

The line clicked into connection and I heard Sandy's voice. "Leo?"

"Yeah, Sandy. Is Sam there?"

No answer. "Jesus, Sandy, how hard can that be? She's either there or she's not."

More silence, then, "Yeah, she's here, Leo. I'm not sure she'll talk to you, though. Hold on a minute."

I leaned back against the pillow, closed my eyes, and kneaded my forehead.

The phone exploded in my ear. "Where were you? You said you'd be there first thing in the morning. I waited for you, but no, something else was more important than me. So, yes, thank you, I had the D&C. And yes, I'm fine. How kind of you to ask. You bastard.''

"Sam, I called. I tried to get in touch with you. I couldn't be there."

"Oh really? Why not? Arnie have another goddamn there's-nobody-else-who-can-help-me-but-you job? And don't give me any shit about how he was there for you. If anybody's been there for you, Leo, it's me. Day in and day out. But that doesn't seem to rate, does it? What should I have done, Leo, worn a gun to bed? Slept back to back so we could cover each other's ass?"

"Arnie's dead, Sam."

That shut her the hell up.

"What do you mean, he's dead?"

"Dead. Murdered. Whoever attacked you went after him first and killed him. I found out about it when I left the hospital. I decided to stay away from anybody close to me. That's why I had that nurse-bodyguard put in your room. I tried to reach you a bunch of times and tell you all this but you were never in."

"Have you called Randi?"

"Yes. She's in hiding, too. Until this is over."

"What is 'this,' Leo?"

"I don't know yet. I spent all day trying to figure it out. I know some of what's going on, but not enough."

"Not enough for what?"

"Enough to go to the police with. Enough to come out of hiding. Enough to identify who attacked you. Take your pick."

"So, what are you going to do?"

"I'm going to lay low and do what I know how to do, be a detective. Try to figure out what's going on."

"And until then? What about us?"

"I don't think we should get together. Right now he doesn't know where I am and he doesn't know where you are. I want it to stay that way. I don't want you exposed to any danger until this is over."

"And how long is that?"

"I don't know, Sam. I wish I did. A few days, probably. I'm not going to spend the rest of my life hiding from this guy. It will end. And soon."

"That's great. You know, this morning I really needed you there. Right now, for the life of me, I can't figure out why."

"Sam, I'm sorry. If there was any way I could have been there, I would have. It's just too risky right now."

"Fine. Whatever." She was too disgusted even to fight with me.

"Look, you're pissed off at me. I let you down. I'm sorry. There's nothing more I can do about it now. You want to let me have it, fine. Save it up until we get together. Do it in person. Until then, I need to know that you're safe from this guy. Please don't go back to the house, or my office, or any of your usual places. I don't know how much information this guy picked up about you while he was in the house. Will you do that?"

"Yes. I'll stay away from those places. Okay?"

"Thanks. Can I have somebody stay there with you?"

"What? One of Rocky's people?"

"Yes."

"No. Absolutely not. I don't want any part of that world near me. I'm fine. I'm safe. You said so yourself. I'm with a friend. I don't need anyone else, thank you."

"Okay. I'll call every day. So we can talk."

"Leo, don't promise me anything. Your track record isn't so hot these days."

I held on to the phone, reluctant to say goodbye, to let things end on such a sorry note, but I couldn't think of any words to turn it around.

"Well, goodnight," I said finally.

"Goodnight, Leo."

I held on, waiting for the click.

"Leo?"

"Yes?"

"I'm sorry about Arnie."

"Yeah. Thanks. Goodnight."

I told no one that I loved her and hung up the already dead phone.

17

I left a message with my service around midnight and then closed my eyes for just a second. Nine hours later my beeper woke me up. I looked at the number and sat up in bed. A quick check confirmed that I smelled bad, and felt worse. I stripped off my clothes and threw them on a chair. I showered and considered shaving, but decided to keep the beard-in-progress for no good reason.

Fresh clothes helped enormously. I sat on the side of the bed and dialed the office.

"Hello."

"Good morning, Kelly. You called me a bit ago."

"Uh-huh. I followed up on the key to the storage locker. It was taken out last week by a Mr. Terence Onslow, listed at 13013 Newminster Road, apartment number 702."

I wrote down the address and phone number as she gave them to me.

"Detective Rhodasson called again. I told him I'd give you the message."

"And so you have. I'll take care of it."

"Are you coming in today?"

"No, I'm not. Any problems?"

"No. Mr. Franklin called, that's all. He wanted to know if I'd heard from you."

"I'll call him. Anything else?"

"No."

"Okay, thanks. I'll be in touch."

I dialed Rocky Franklin's home and sent Tawni scurrying to get him.

"Leo, what's going on? I heard that Sam fired the minder you wanted to watch her."

"Yeah, but it's okay. She's laying low too."

"Do you have any idea who attacked her?"

"Yeah, I even have some leads on why. It's a stolen data disk. I'm having the disk analyzed right now. She was attacked because the guy thought Arnie and I stole this disk from him."

"How did you get it?"

"Long story short, it was planted on us. The guy who attacked Sam ambushed Arnie and killed him, then came looking for me. Sam was just in the way."

"You need some help on this?"

"Yeah. I want somebody to keep an eye on Sam. Nothing close or obvious. Just a shadow. And no connection to me or the office. She doesn't want it, so they have to be able to watch her without her knowing it."

"No problem. I'll get someone from Dickie Pruitt's outfit."

"Thanks."

"Anything else?"

"Not now. Maybe later. Rocky, I don't know when I'm going to be back in the office. Maybe you should put somebody else in charge. Between this and the Babcock thing I haven't been much use lately."

"Don't worry about it. I'm going to put Frank Martell in until you get this cleared up. Then the job is still yours. Babcock could have happened to anyone. I think you handled it just fine. We'll survive. Our reputation is still good and I think that's because you didn't try to cover it up or make excuses. This trouble you've got is personal. If I canned people because they had troubles in their lives, what kind of boss would I be? Don't answer that. Do what you have to do and keep me informed."

"Thanks, Rocky. I really appreciate that."

I called Rhodasson. He wasn't in, so I left my name and the office number. I did my part.

I drove through Vienna toward Tysons Corner and stopped at a local diner for breakfast. I couldn't remember my last meal. The food there was excellent, the portions huge and the prices prehistoric. That helped get past the exposed pipe and chipped linoleum decor, and the fanged waitress.

I ordered some S.O.S. and a cup of coffee. Two booths away I watched a huge construction worker shovel his breakfast into his face. He ate with metronomic efficiency, stopping only when enough food had collected around his mouth that he could wipe his face with his toast. When my food arrived I ate quickly, but with an eye for my neighbors.

From there I went to Onslow's apartment. The buildings on Newminster Road are done in early poorhouse. Identical red-brick blocks with sloping metal roofs on them like dunce caps. Each one with row after row of tiny windows to ration the sunlight. A tad less imagination and they would have been invisible. Instead they were just hideous.

Terence Onslow's building faced poorhouse number five. I took the elevator up and followed the arrows to his apartment. I knocked until I was sure no one was home. A quick check of the hallway and I pulled out my lockpicks. Ninety seconds of coaxing and I was inside. I locked the door behind me. Onslow's apartment was immaculate. The kitchen was all smooth surfaces and closed cupboards. Nothing, not even a toaster or a coffee maker, was on the counters. The white sofa and glass coffee table told me that he didn't have kids or a dog. There were three wicker chairs around the dining table. The fourth was in front of the electric range. I walked into the kitchen and saw a skillet on the range. I picked it up. Bits of meat still clung to the pan. I was looking at the print of a human hand.

I put the pan down, pulled the chair away from the range,

and sat down. No need to hurry. Terence Onslow wasn't coming back.

A couple of deep breaths cleared my head. Stay frosty, Leo, or you'll be next. That was all the motivation I needed. I stood up, pulled out my pocket recorder, and began to make notes.

No struggle. Onslow knew him? Surprised? Grabbed outside? Door had no dead bolt. Did he get in like me? Onslow had the disk. How did he know that? What's their connection? Tortured Onslow to get location. Got key for locker. Why put disk in locker? Onslow dead? Yeah, or still being held until the man gets the disk. Maybe he needs him to analyze it, like I need Reed. I clicked off the recorder, got a towel from a kitchen drawer, and began to search the apartment.

I was pretty sure Onslow was dead, so I focused on information about his past. His interest in science fiction and bondage magazines was no use to me. He wouldn't be out buying any new ones. I knew nothing about the man until I went through the desk in his bedroom. The center drawer had an address book and checkbook. I pocketed those. The top side drawer had recent credit card slips, canceled checks, and payroll stubs. I glanced through them all and put them in my jacket. The deep file drawer had tax returns, insurance policies, warranties, and information about his car. There was nothing unusual in any of the files, so I left them after noting the make of the car and its tag number.

I wiped away any trace of my visit and put the towel in my other pocket.

In the car, I checked the address for my next stop: BMR Inc., Terence Onslow's employers.

18

BMR sat midway up a hill overlooking an auto park. Down below, fifteen automobile dealers were clustered on both sides of the road, eagerly playing their version of grand theft auto. For most people, buying a car is like playing the shell game at a pickpockets' convention. It's a shame because ten minutes of homework and the willingness to walk away will give you the upper hand.

BMR was a dark green mirrored cube. I watched myself walk up to the entrance, and saw no one I wanted to know.

The security guard at the front desk was a paunchy black man with a fringe of tight white curls.

"I'd like to see Mr. Terence Onslow."

He consulted a directory, then pushed a number on his phone. No answer. He dialed another number.

"Is Mr. Onslow here, Marcia?" He listened, then turned to me.

"I'm sorry, Mr. Onslow is not here. The secretary said he's been gone for about a week. He had to go home. There was a death in the family."

Cute. Somebody had a twisted sense of humor. "I'd like to speak to Mr. Onslow's supervisor, then."

"And you are?"

"Leo Haggerty, private investigator."

He dialed another number and tried to sell someone on the idea of talking to me.

"Ms. Hornyak will talk to you. She's Dr. Shatzkin's secretary. Mr. Onslow worked for Dr. Shatzkin. Why don't you have a seat. She'll be right down."

"Thanks."

I looked at the lobby chairs; armless, tubular metal squiggles that doubled back on themselves for support. No thanks. The green tint of the glass put a permanent verdant cast on the landscaping around the building.

Other consulting firms dotted the hillside. Tysons Corner is the Virginia headquarters for the "Beltway Bandits," consulting firms of scientists whose arcane knowledge the government thinks it desperately needs and ex-government officials who know how to massage the swollen teats on the giant sow of procurement.

The car dealers down below were rank amateurs at the alchemy of turning bullshit into gold.

"Excuse me. Mr. Haggerty?"

I turned to face Ms. Hornyak. She slipped me one of those soft, curved flippers, from the age of the kiss on bended knee, that you can't shake, even gently. I let her have it back.

"I'm Alison Hornyak, Dr. Shatzkin's secretary. How may I help you?"

"I'm a private investigator, Ms. Hornyak. I've been looking into the activities of Mr. Terence Onslow. I'd like to know what kind of work he did at BMR."

"What are you investigating? Do you think it involves BMR?"

"It could. It's too soon to tell."

Ms. Hornyak compressed her lips in thought. She was tall, plain, and myopic. Thick glasses hung from a strap around her neck. Her features were good: clear gray eyes, a straight nose, high forehead and cheekbones, full lips. Her brown hair was limp and piled upon her shoulders like poorly hung drapes. A shapeless business suit didn't flatter her. She made me think of the women I'd met at my twenty-year high school reunion who were so much more attractive than they'd been as girls. One of them told me the secret. They weren't being dressed by their mothers anymore. Maybe Ms. Hornyak still lived at home.

"I'm not at liberty to tell you anything specific, Mr. Haggerty. However, I think Dr. Schatzkin would like to talk to you. Will you follow me?"

She turned and led me through a set of double doors, down a hall, up an elevator, through another set of doors marked Authorized Personnel Only, to an office door. The nameplate read Robert Schatzkin, M.D., Ph.D.

Ms. Hornyak knocked and opened the door.

"Dr. Schatzkin, this is Leo Haggerty, a private investigator. He's looking into Terry Onslow's background. He thinks it might affect BMR."

Schatzkin pointed to a seat facing his desk. "Thank you, Alison.

"I'd like to see some identification, Mr. Haggerty."

I showed him my license and gave him one of my cards. "What do you want to know, Mr. Haggerty?"

"First, what kind of work does Terry Onslow do for you?"

"He's a computer operator for us, that's all. He enters and analyzes data we receive from field trial physicians."

"Does he have access to anything vital or secret that you are doing?"

"No. He isn't one of the research team. Just a data processor."

"I understand that he's been gone for a week now. A death in the family."

"Could be. I really don't know. If so, I think it shows that Mr. Onslow's position here could be easily filled. We haven't missed a beat."

"What does BMR do, Doctor?"

"We're a biomedical research firm. We have a number of different projects going."

"What about this one? The one Terry Onslow was on?"

"This project is looking at combinations of anti-viral and immuno-modulators to try to stop the transfer of the HIV virus from infected mothers to their fetuses."

I scribbled notes in my notebook. Schatzkin leaned back in his chair. He had on one of those ridiculous toupees that look like a roadkill. His face was dominated by a hook nose and thick, plum-colored lips. To boot, he was as thin as last year's dead.

"Let me ask you a question, Mr. Haggerty. Why are you investigating Mr. Onslow?"

"I'm sorry, that's confidential, Doctor. It's just a routine background check, that's all."

"He's been offered a job elsewhere? Is that it?"

"I'm sorry, Doctor, I don't know."

"Why do you think it might affect BMR?"

"Mr. Onslow has been connected to a couple of individuals of dubious reputation, shall we say. I told Ms. Hornyak that it might affect BMR before I knew what his position was. He seems so peripheral to the project that it's hard to see how he could compromise your work."

"Well, I think you're probably right. Terry was not privy to the design of the study, nor did he know what compounds we were testing. I don't see how he had knowledge that could hurt us."

Schatzkin looked quite relieved now that he'd convinced himself there was nothing to worry about.

"Thank you for taking time to speak with me. I can find my way out."

"You're welcome." We shook hands and Schatzkin was poring over a journal before I closed the door.

On the way out, I passed Alison Hornyak's desk. I stopped and handed her my card.

"If you hear anything about Terry Onslow, you know, gossip, rumors floating around the office, would you please give me a call?"

Ms. Hornyak took my card and fixed me with a stare like I'd suggested an unnatural sex act. I smiled and turned away. I'd gone three steps when I returned to her desk.

"You said that Mr. Onslow had gone home to attend a family funeral. Can you tell me where he was from? I'd like to try to talk with him by phone."

"I'm sorry, I don't have that information. You might check with Personnel. They're one floor down, at the far end of the hall."

"Thank you."

I introduced myself to Talisha Scoggins of Personnel. Every strand of her corn-rowed hair ended in a bright bead. When she spun around in her chair to face me, her hair flew like a carnival ride. As the ride ended she topped it with an incandescent smile. "Can I help you?"

"I hope so. I'm a private investigator trying to locate Terry Onslow. Do you know him?"

"Yeah, sure. He's been out. Family funeral, I think."

"How long has he been gone?"

"Couple of days, I guess. Why?"

"You like Terry Onslow?"

"Yeah. He's a nice guy. Why?"

"I think something's happened to him. Something bad. Why don't you check his time sheets. I'll bet he's been gone at least a week. Pretty long for a funeral, huh?"

"He could have stayed to help out his family."

"Okay. But he'd call, right, to let a supervisor know, to make a change on his leave slips. I'll bet you nobody's heard from him."

"I don't know . . ."

"Tell you what, if I'm wrong, I'll drop it right here. You don't have to say a thing. Punch it up on your screen. See for yourself."

Talisha turned to her computer. I thought about grabbing a bead as it went by and climbing aboard.

Two minutes went by. She looked at her screen, then tapped

out other codes and studied what came up. When she turned back, she wasn't smiling.

"Okay. You're right. He's been gone for six work days. He was switched to leave without pay last Wednesday. The computer supervisor for the project sent a letter out on Friday. I read the letter. It said that unless Terry returned his calls or checked in by Friday, he'd be fired. What do you want to know?"

"I want to know everything I can about the guy. Do you know who his friends were?"

"No, but I can find out pretty easily. The computer support staff for that project isn't too large. If he didn't hang out with somebody there, they'd know who he did spend time with."

"Great. Here's my card. If you locate someone who knew Terry well or who can put me in touch with such a person, call the beeper number, any time, day or night. Tell them I'll pay for the information. That includes you."

I slipped out my wallet and put two twenties on her desk. "That's a down payment. I'll match it for anything I can use." Talisha looked infinitesimally insulted but slipped the money into her desk drawer.

In my car, I called Reed Lewis.

"Hello, Reed. Tell me that you know everything about that data disk."

"Okay, I know everything about that data disk."

"I hate when you do that."

"I know. But it's the only reasonable reply to your absurd request."

"Point well taken. Do you know anything about what's on the disk?"

"Not yet, Leo. When I find the right program to crunch the numbers, I'll know something. Until then, nothing. Do you know anything about whose disk it is?"

"Yeah. His name is Terry Onslow. He works in the computer support services for a company called BMR Incorporated. Do you know them?"

"No, but I can find out what computers and software they use. Most companies try to stay with the same programs for their basic functions. It keeps their costs down. Those programs should tell me what statistical analysis package to use. Do you know what kind of project he was on?"

"He was entering data and analyzing it on field trials from physicians using various combinations of, wait a minute" —I flipped open my notebook—"anti-virals and immuno-modulators on transmission of HIV from infected mothers to fetus. How does that help you?"

"Hey, Leo, you call me for stuff you don't know. I call other people for things I don't know. I've got friends who are free-lance consultants to biomed firms. I'll make some calls. Ask them what the data looks like for those kinds of studies."

"Great. Looks like we're closing in on it. Call me as soon as you have something."

"Can I get back to my work, please?"

"Silly me, keeping you like this."

19

Back at the Bed-a-Bye, I played telephone tag with Rhodasson, checked in with the office, and waited. What did Terry Onslow have that was worth killing him, Bonnie, and Arnie for? He was a computer operator on a medical research project. An anonymous number cruncher. It couldn't have been something routine to the job because he was being replaced. Now if someone wiped out the whole support team, I'd have something there. It had to be something unusual he knew, something he did differently from other people in the pool. Unless he was a genius and saw things everybody else missed, it had to be something he came across accidentally or otherwise that no one else saw. Something in the numbers. Something so glaring that even if he didn't know what the study was, or what the data meant, he knew it was hot.

I looked at the copies of *Call to Arms* I'd taken from Snipes's house. Maybe there'd be something useful in there. Like a letter to the editor from my unknown adversary, with his home address.

I piled up the pillows, lay down, and started reading.

The first issue had an article by Professor Herbert Schneckerl, Ph.D., head of the Institute for Race Studies, that explained to me how niggers were the result of breeding between African

Jews and baboons. That accounted for the physical and sexual prowess of the nigger, owing to his recent descent from the apes. The nigger, it went on, was all appetite and no brains, while the Jew was the opposite. Alone, neither one was the equal of the thoughtfully virile, white Christian male. Fascinating stuff this. Dr. Schneckerl went on to explain how the nigger was actually the Jews' "Golem," a mindless brute sent to corrupt and destroy the "New Jerusalem" of white America. The nigger's rampant sexuality created a horde of brainless apes led around by their dicks. In the background the cowardly Jew, craven but cunning, stood waiting to take over America after the firestorm of nigger revolution. What was to be done? I could hardly wait for the answer, which was promised in the next issue. I flipped through the magazine looking for anything of use, then threw it away.

I picked up the next issue and there was Dr. Schneckerl's face. Curly corn-silk hair, bland round face, fixed smile, and empty blue eyes. Alfred E. Newman on PCP.

Ah, the solution. The gift from God to his white Christian children: the cleansing plague of AIDS. Its main victims were homosexuals. Everyone knew that the Jews had an extraordinarily high percentage of queers, owing to the frigidity of their women and their own perverse desires. How could you expect a race that rejected Christ not to be perverted in every fashion? A sidebar promised a theological analysis of homosexuality as a sign of Satanic possession. After all, wasn't the Osculum Infamae, the kiss of shame demanded by Satan, actually analingus as foreplay to being buggered by him?

The other main group of victims, intravenous drug users, were overwhelmingly black, or their brown cousins, the spick. Both were unable to tolerate frustration and work for their rewards in this life like the noble white Christian man and woman. So they gave in to the immediate physical pleasures of drugs; and because of their lack of will, an obviously missing higher mental function, they became addicted. This plague of AIDS would cleanse America of the pestilence of the nigger and the kike. Dr. Schneckerl concluded sadly, though, that while the nigger population would be much smaller, it probably wouldn't be entirely eradicated, and that the ultimate menace was still the sly old Jew always waiting to bring down the clean, pure, white Christian.

Scheckerl closed with a group of bizarre recommendations on how to protect yourself from accidental infection by any racially impure people.

I went through the rest until I came to a picture of a man hanging impaled on a barbed wire while German shepherds tore him to pieces. In the background guards smoked and smiled. The caption read "Christmas Dinner, 1943." I tore the magazine in half and threw the pieces across the room.

I scooped up the other magazines and tossed them into the trashcan. Something slipped out of one of them. I picked up four photographs of a black woman having sex with two white men. There were no markings on the back.

There's a pure, white, Christian motive if I ever saw one, Harold. Let's kill the men so we can fuck their women. Run that one past Jesus and let me know what he says.

20

I lay there waiting for my beeper to go off, like the timer on a roast. Then I could climb out of my pan and do something useful. No such luck.

I found my magic wand and pointed it at the TV set. Each channel annoyed me more than the one before. After a couple of laps around the dial, I settled on a music video show. The host was groveling before an infuriatingly successful rock star. If he got his nose any further up his guest's ass, he'd have to breathe through his ears.

They took turns masturbating each other's egos on national television and then introduced a hot new band that "El Supremo" had discovered. I counted the number of superlatives in the introduction and concluded—according to the second law of hype, which states that the number of superlatives is inversely related to their meaning—that this band couldn't plug in their amps.

Thirty seconds of confirmation was all I could stand. I lay there but could not rest. I felt like I had poison ivy in my veins.

This was a dangerous time. My mind wasn't focused. There was no telling where it might wander off to. Somewhere out there, in the tall grass of life, there was a hole of grief. If I wasn't careful, if I didn't look where I was going, I was going to fall right into it. And maybe just not come out for a while. But that was a luxury I couldn't afford right now. If my foe caught me there, he'd pull the earth up over me and I'd never get out.

I pushed off the bed and went into the bathroom. I splashed some water on my face and took a reading in the mirror. My hair rose up like a stand of sea oats. No way could I invest this stubble with any cachet. Bloodshot eyes and a two-thousand-yard stare just added to my charm.

There was nothing else for me to do except unpack. I'd put it off as long as I could. It was a surrender to the idea that I'd be here a while.

My dop kit was already in the bathroom. That just left some clothes to put in the dresser. When I finished that, I put the suitcase on the small table and threw the dirty clothes into it. When I was down to my last change, I'd take the dirty stuff out to the dumpster, trash it, buy new, and start over. Laundry was another luxury I didn't have time for.

I pulled Sam's photo out of the side pocket and propped it up on the desk. That picture was almost five years old. There were strands of gray in her hair and crow's feet in the corners of her eyes, but she was just as beautiful as the day I met her. When I was young, I'd see a beautiful woman and wonder if she was passionate, too. Now I knew that a passionate woman is always beautiful.

She never called sex "making love." She wasn't sure what love had to do with it. The way we went at each other, she said, it was more like making fire. Tinder and flint. Flint and tinder.

I ran my hand over the picture. Her hair didn't move. She didn't smile.

My beeper went off and brought me back from the edge of reverie. The pull was strong, into memory, desire, and regret. They had powerful claims to lay. Claims I could not ignore forever. Some day I would not fight them, but not now, not here.

21

I dialed the number on the beeper. A woman's voice answered.

"This is Leo Haggerty. I'm returning your call. Who is this?"

"Oh. My name is Ellen Moffatt. Talisha Scoggins said you were looking for Terry Onslow, something about him being away at a family funeral."

"That's right. Do you know Terry?"

"Yes I do. We work in support services for Dr. Schatzkin's project. Talisha said you wanted some information about Terry. Can I ask why?"

"Sure. I don't think Terry's at a family funeral. I think he's in deep trouble. I'm a private investigator and I came across Terry's name while investigating some very bad people. I think they might have him. That's why he isn't at work."

"That can't be right. Terry is as quiet a guy as you can imagine. I don't think he'd know how to get in trouble."

"I wish that were true, Ms. Moffatt, but I don't think so. How well did you know Terry Onslow?"

"Not really well. I don't think anybody at work did. We talked in the office. Ate lunch together sometimes. Every once in a while he'd come out with us after work over to Clyde's or the American Café. But he wasn't a party animal, that's for sure. Mr. Neat and Tidy, we called him."

"Why?"

"Terry is a neat freak. His workstation was always immaculate. He'd never even loosen his tie when we were out."

"What kind of worker was he?"

"I guess the company was happy with him. He was real punctual. Worked a full eight hours."

"I guess I mean did he have any unusual skills, something he was particularly good at, something he did differently from other members of your group?"

"Well, Terry was pretty much our troubleshooter. He was real good at debugging programs when problems showed up. He was real patient and real detail-oriented. So he was good at finding glitches and fixing them."

"Was there anything he did that no one else in the pool did?" There was silence. "Ms. Moffatt?"

"Yes. Look, I don't want to get in trouble. You aren't working for BMR, are you?"

"No. Absolutely not. Look, I have no interest in getting anyone in trouble. I'm trying to get Terry Onslow *out* of some trouble. What do you know?"

More silence. "Please, Ms. Moffatt, Ellen, I think Terry's in the kind of trouble that gets you dead. What do you know?"

"Okay. Terry did one thing that nobody else did. He worked nights on computer security."

"Okay. So what's the problem?"

"Well, everybody in the pool was supposed to rotate that job. But we all hated it. We've all got families. All of us except Terry. Like I said, he wasn't big on going out nights. So we worked out a deal where we logged in nights as if we were there but let Terry stay late to watch things. Then each paycheck we'd pay him for the overtime. It wasn't like no one was doing the job. Terry was there. God, he was better at that stuff than any of us. Watching those screens used to drive me crazy. Nothing ever happened."

"Tell me about this security job. What did he have to do?"

"Do you know anything about Dr. Schatzkin's research?"

"Only a little. He's testing drugs to block the transfer of AIDS from mothers to the fetus."

"Right. Well, we have doctors all over the country testing a variety of compounds. These doctors put their data on our system from their offices, or the hospitals. Some of them are in California, so they put data on, you know, like two or three hours after we close up here. So there has to be someone here to make sure that it all goes in right. Answer any questions the doctors might have. Fix problems. It's right up Terry's alley. All this data stays in what we call a buffer. Then on Fridays it's loaded all at once into the ongoing data of the study."

"Why did you say he worked on computer security? I don't see the security part of this."

"Well, that's what Dr. Schatzkin calls it. After all the problems his project has had, he's gotten pretty hyper about things."

"What kind of problems?"

"Well, first there were the GLPs and blacklist calls."

"What are GLPs?"

"Good Laboratory Procedures. Someone was calling the FDA and telling them he wasn't using good lab procedures. So we had investigators all over the place."

"Was he?"

"Absolutely. He's a by-the-numbers guy. Very scrupulous. We run so many analyses on his data they scream when we boot them up."

"What about blacklists?"

"Oh, there was a call that we had a blacklisted researcher on staff. Someone the FDA has caught cheating before. That was just a nuisance call."

"Any other problems?"

"We got a crank call that said we had a virus in the data. That really freaked Dr. Schatzkin out. He shut everything down. Called in outside consultants. They found nothing. We were afraid he was going to fire us all, just to be sure. Start over with new people. I guess he decided it was some prank. We always thought it was a con by these computer consultants to drum up business. Call in a virus, then come by to check out the system for plenty of money. You know there's nothing there, so it's easy money."

"When did all this happen?"

"A while ago. Four or five months, maybe. Then it all stopped. I don't know when. We haven't heard anything for a couple of months, I guess."

"When did Terry start doing the security work every night?"

"About six weeks ago."

"Who's doing it now? One person? Or are you all rotating it?"

"To tell you the truth, nobody is. We figured we'd just let Terry keep doing it when he got back."

"In case Terry doesn't come back, you'd better get someone on it. Make sure that nothing funny is going on."

"That's a good idea."

"Anything else unusual about this project? Rumors about the staff, anything?"

"Not really. One investigator left, that's all."

"Who's that?"

"Dr. Francis. She came on as part of Dr. Schatzkin's team. It never seemed to work out. So she left."

"What didn't work out?"

"She had her own ideas about what combinations to investigate and she wanted to run her own parallel studies. Dr. Schatzkin told her no. This was his project. He'd designed it and he'd run it his own way."

"What did Dr. Francis do?"

"She threw a fit. Then she sulked, I guess. Coming in late, leaving early. She badmouthed Dr. Schatzkin to everyone. Sounded like a jilted lover, if you ask me."

"Do you think they were lovers?"

"No. Not really. She threw Dr. Schatzkin some cleavage, and some batted eyes. It was pretty funny, actually. He didn't even notice that she wore a skirt. If Schatzkin can't put it under a microscope, he isn't interested."

"So what happened?"

"She went over his head, to the board of directors, to get backing for her own projects. The way I hear it, there was quite a row. Schatzkin made allegations that she'd falsified part of her vita. Something about leaving projects before they were finished. Stealing credit for research papers from students who did all the work, that kind of stuff. Anyway, the board backed Dr. Schatzkin and she quit and went to another lab."

"Where did she go?"

"Another R&D place. I don't remember."

"Was this before the crank calls and so on?"

"Let me see. No, actually they ended before she left. A few weeks, maybe a month before."

"You're sure about that?"

"Yeah, I'm sure. It was before. After she left, things were real quiet. Until this."

"Listen, if I need to, can I get back to you to check some things out?"

"Sure. I hope you're wrong about Terry. He's a nice guy. A little dull, but a nice guy."

"I'll be by tomorrow to drop off the money for your information."

"I didn't call for the money. I called because I was worried about our little thing with Terry and the overtime. I'll straighten that out with everybody tomorrow."

"If you or anyone else sees anything strange with the data, call me at this number. Right away. Okay?" I read off my beeper number.

"Sure."

"Thanks."

"Wait a minute. I've got it."

"Got what?"

"Where Dr. Francis went. She went to Palmetto Research Corporation."

"Where's that?"

"Just up the hill from us."

22

Ellen Moffatt had moved me a bit closer to connecting Terry Onslow with my mystery man. Energized by that bit of progress, I went to the desk and did some homework.

I slipped on my glasses and scribbled some notes in my address book. When I finished, I emptied my jacket onto the desk. I threw Onslow's towel in with the rest of the dirty laundry, and spent the next hour analyzing his check stubs and credit card slips. Nothing. Mr. Neat and Tidy. No strange purchases, enigmatic entries, or puzzling patterns.

I pushed back from the desk and wished for an Irish whiskey. Instead, I set about to pull together what I knew about Onslow, X, and the disk.

Onslow was on the computers at night. He was monitoring the data loading. He saw something happen, something funny in Schatzkin's project. Then what? He approached whoever it was about what he'd seen and they *sicced* X on him. Probably exit Onslow. But he'd obeyed the first commandment of computers: Backup, Backup, Backup. The disk in the locker.

I tried to put some spin on that scenario. Perhaps someone had bought Onslow to spy on the data collection. Keep them informed. A competitor, perhaps? He was their inside man, but he decided to blackmail them. Same ending.

There were no funny payments in Onslow's bank book, but that meant nothing. Maybe we should do a full asset search on him. Surprise, Leo, you can still think like a pro when you have to.

Who would benefit from knowing about Schatzkin's research? Or tampering with it? I'd need to know more about what was on the data disk before I could answer that.

I was starting to flag. I scooped together Onslow's papers and made a stack of them. Tomorrow they'd go in the evidence box in my trunk. I called Sam and got Sandy's answering machine. I held on to see if she'd pick it up, but no one did.

I checked in with my answering service and left a message for the Rev.

Nothing left to do but try to sleep. I got under the blanket, punched the pillow into submission, and lay there. And lay there. Under my blank flagstone face there were beetles and worms, and they loved the dark. It was their time. I'd tried to banish them, to will them away, to will sleep. I might as well have tried to nail a board to the sea.

First thing out from under was Arnie's face. My friend, but so different. For him, life was a test. Honor and courage the subjects. Death the examiner. Nothing else mattered but how you faced it. True as far as it went, but there were other things that mattered. The niche you filled in another's heart that helped them face life. A life rich with pleasure was not incompatible with honor and courage. Perhaps it eroded it, compromised it. Arnie had little to lose when he died. He wore his life lightly, and stepped from it easily. He faced death well but skimped on life, tasting few of its pleasures.

I drank more deeply, and I was afraid. Afraid to die, afraid to leave all this behind. I would need more courage to live, to live with this fear. Maybe more courage than I had.

Why had I gone with him? We were friends. He needed me. That was only part of it. I never thought it would come to this. I believed in his charmed presence. Nothing ever touched him. We would get close to the edge. One more time, for old time's sake. We would dance close with death. Hold her cheek to cheek. Step lightly together. Spin, dip, and slip away, flushed but safe.

One time too many, Leo, one time too many. I wasn't like Arnie. I was connected. To him, to Randi, to Sam. I'd drawn and quartered myself. The only question left was when the horses bolted, where would the pieces fall?

23

My beeper went off and I groped for it on the nightstand. Reed Lewis's number. I reached for the phone and dialed it.

"Good morning, Leo," he crooned.

"Is it? What have you got?" I sat up and pulled my .45 out from under the pillow.

"I think I know what this guy Onslow found and what he did with it."

I waited. "Yeah?"

"It's too complicated to do over the phone, Leo. You have to come over so I can show it to you. I also did some homework with a couple of guys who do a lot of biomed programming. Maybe it'll be helpful to you."

"On my way, Reed." I hung up and got dressed.

Onslow's papers went in the trunk. Then I stopped at a McDonald's and got a couple of breakfast McSomethings and a McCoffee.

I knocked on Reed's door, and when he opened it, marched in holding breakfast high.

"Have you eaten?"

"Yeah, but thanks. Sit down. I want to show you what was on that disk."

Reed picked up a sheaf of papers and handed half to me. I

sat down, unpacked, and set the food aside. He had his copy of the papers in his hands.

"Okay. You have two different sorts of information there. Pages one to six are raw data files. At least that's what my friends think. You were right about the first column. Those nine-digit numbers are Social Security numbers. Probably doctors, turning in data on field trials. The second column, see where it says '01' for every one, that's the group for the data. Drug tests are done double-blind. No one, except the original researcher, knows who has been assigned to what drug and who has a placebo. That removes experimenter bias in measuring and reporting data.

"Look at the data. There's five blocks. Five compounds being studied, or four and a placebo. Okay. The rest of the columns are variables in the subjects, lab results, blood tests—I can't tell. Only someone who knows the study can tell you what they refer to. The last column is the date the data was entered. These batches are entered on Fridays. See, page one's data is September ninth, page two is the sixteenth, and so on. You with me?"

I nodded.

"All right. Flip to page seven. These pages are analyses based on that raw data. Once I figured out that this was medical research, the reports became clear. They're laid out in the standard report format required by the FDA for drug testing. Now the columns have headings that mean something. Look across the top: means, standard deviations, and so on. The last column is the important one. It says $t > .05$ and those asterisks. Those are the significant values. Wherever there's an asterisk or two, there's a statistically significant value."

It must have been my labored breathing that gave me away. Reed put down his papers and smiled at me.

"You never took statistics, did you?"

I hung my head.

"Or multivariate research design?"

My chin was on my chest.

"Okay. Here's the mega-maxi compressed version for men of action. The purpose of controlled research is to reject, if possible, the null hypothesis." Reed waited to see if my eyeballs crossed, then went on. "Which is whether a difference between groups, in this case the drugs and the placebo, is due to chance rather than an actual difference in effectiveness. Okay, scientists pick cut-off values that they feel are significantly greater than chance, to determine which results are valid. Here it's >.05. The difference between a drug and the placebo has to be greater than what would occur at the .05 level or one in twenty cases to be statistically significant as a sign of the efficacy of the drug."

I nodded.

"Okay. Let's go to pages thirteen through twenty-four. This is what's on the second set of files. It's almost identical to what's on the first set. Except for two things. Look at the last page. See where there are those asterisks for the data on group two from the third week on? Now flip to page twenty-four. No asterisks. I went back to the raw data and compared them. The data in these files have been degraded by ten percent across the board. The end result of a statistical analysis is no difference between groups."

"English, please, Reed. I'm bleeding from the ears."

"Right. English. The data in the first set of files says that compound two has a statistically significant effect. The data on the second group of files says that no compound has a statistically significant effect. Now remember that doesn't mean clinical effectiveness, just statistical. Compound two is better than a placebo, or any of the others, and it's not by chance. But it may not make you better."

"So what's the point?"

"The point is you focus your efforts on number two. You refine it. Then run studies with varying dosages until you hit one that's clinically effective. That's your therapeutic dosage. If you don't have horrendous side effects, you have a marketable, effective, safe drug."

"So which of the files is the real data?"

"Why thank you for asking. Flip to page twenty-five. This is where it gets interesting."

"You're really enjoying yourself, aren't you?" I said.

"Absolutely. This last stuff is not data, per se. This first page is an activity log. Anybody who wanted to get into this data base has to be an approved user. Now my friends tell me that medical research security is generally horrendous, not at all like military or financial systems. So, what we're looking at is unusual. Did the project have some troubles? Virus threats?"

"Yeah. So what's unusual?" I sipped the coffee and took a bite out of the sandwich.

"Well, they've got a callback system. You need an approved phone number to get on the system. You punch it in and the computer calls you back at the number to confirm that it's actually the approved line. Then it lets you enter your identification number. If that's approved, you're in. They must do a lot of data collecting and so on with modems, so these doctors can phone it in from their offices.

"Anyway, column one is phone numbers. Column two is user identification numbers. See, it's the Social Security numbers. Then the date and time they logged on and off. The last columns are cpu time, I/O amounts, disk-space usage, connect time, resource utilization. This is from a big system running a lot of projects. The company would use these figures to bill people by department or project for their computer usage.

"Okay, our boy, Terry Onslow, went through this activity log and he got curious about one person. Look halfway down. Phone number 555-1097, then the I.D. number. He did a sort of all the files that person had been into, and guess what he found?"

"Reed, please?"

"Okay. He found two directories for this I.D. number. Look at the first. The I.D. number is the same, but it's a different phone number. This directory is a secretary's. Tons of correspondence. Mostly word-processing stuff. But there's also the

555-1097 number. It's also logged out to the same I.D. number and has a directory. But there's only a few files in it."

I flicked the paper. "This stuff?"

"You got it right the first time."

"Okay, Onslow was on the computer after hours. He was helping the doctors load their data, running the weekly analyses of what was already there, and he sees something. What?"

"Look at the time and utilization for this person. Way beyond anyone else logging in data in this project. More than a secretary would need. She's using lots of disk space and storage, lots of CPU time. So he goes to see what she's doing. Maybe he's bored and curious, or he takes his job seriously. Who knows? He finds these directories. One makes sense, one doesn't. He punches up the funny one, and if he's been doing the data analyses for this project it wouldn't be hard for him to see the difference."

"I'll bet you your Redskins tickets that the data everybody else is looking at is the insignificant version."

"So they've got a drug that works, or might, and they don't know it."

"Right again, Sherlock. They'll run the study to its conclusion and then scrap it."

I closed my eyes and tried to imagine scenarios for the data. A secretary and Onslow were in it together? No, why would he need her? He was perfectly positioned to do it all by himself.

So Onslow caught her at something. There goes my insider theory, too. He wasn't in on it. At least not initially.

That leaves blackmail gone sour, or Onslow knew too much and had to be silenced. But why a secretary? A disgruntled employee acting on her own? What's the motive? Maybe someone else bought her? Who?

I thought about the asset search on Onslow. He wasn't going to get rich squeezing a secretary. No, she was either the key herself or she knew who was. Either way she was a step closer to the center than Onslow. I had a hard time with a secretary hiring a killer to retrieve the disk, not for herself at least. But she could peddle it to another lab. That's where the money would be.

When all else fails, Rocky used to say, look for love or money, or better yet both. The twin engines for almost all crimes: empty pockets and broken hearts.

X smelled of money. Big money, to take the chances he did. No, the secretary wasn't the end of the chain. There was at least one somebody in the shadows behind her.

I opened my eyes. "I'm sorry, Reed. I was trying to see where all this took me. Thanks, man. You've really helped a lot. I owe you one. A big one."

"True, and I fervently hope that I don't ever have to use it."

"I've got to run. There's things I need to do with this information."

"Sure. Just don't forget these." Reed handed me two disks.

"What's this?"

"A backup. People are getting killed for this thing, remember. Put the second one in a safe place. You might need it."

"Good point." I pocketed them both and slipped the printouts into an envelope Reed gave me.

24

I sat in my car and dialed the BMR number from the disk.

"Sally Boszik's desk."

"Sally Boszik, please."

"I'm sorry. She's not at her desk. Can I take a message?"

"No, that's okay. I'll call back."

I called information and got her home number and address. That wasn't the 555 number, either. Okay, it's not her home number or her office. Where does she call from?

I dialed the number directly. What the hell. Maybe an answering machine would say, "Corporate Espionage Services. I'm sorry all of our spies are busy now. If you'll leave your alias and the number of a pay phone near you, we'll get right back to you." Actually, it just rang ten times and I hung up.

I called Kelly at the office.

"Franklin Investigations."

"Good morning, Kelly. It's Leo. How's it going with Frank Martell? Go ahead, tell me it's awful and you can't wait for me to come back."

"Boy, am I glad you called."

"What is it?"

"We got a strange call last night, and again this morning."

McBreakfast hardened in my gut and I exhaled slowly. "Go ahead, what was it?"

"It was a man. Both times. Last night, he called and left a number where you could call him back. This morning he called again."

"What did he say?"

"Just a second. I wrote it all down. I didn't say a thing, I just listened."

"You did the right thing. Read it to me."

"He said, 'I want to talk to Leo Haggerty.' I told him you weren't in the office and he said he'd call back at noon today. It was a matter of life and death. He wouldn't leave his name."

"Okay. At noon when he calls, put him on hold, get me on my beeper, and I'll call in and make it a conference call."

"Okay. Is there anything else you want done? Frank wanted to know."

"Just remember to set up your recorder on that line and tape the conversation. I do need something right now, though."

"Okay."

"Go get the reverse directories for the metropolitan area. I need an address for a phone number."

Kelly came back and asked for the number. I gave it to her and held on as she flipped through the books.

"No entry. Could be a new line, or it's unlisted and unpublished."

"I've got a feeling that it's the latter. Okay, thanks. I'll be waiting for your call at noon."

"Right. Oh, one other thing, Leo."

"Yeah."

"Hurry back. Frank has all the pencils on your desk arranged by length."

"Soon. Soon."

I put the phone down and took a few minutes to concoct another adventure for my wandering psychotic patient. Then I dialed Directory Assistance.

"What city, please?"

"I don't know. Fairfax County."

"The name?"

"Uh, I don't know. My name is Frank Martell. My sister just called me. She was hysterical but she wouldn't tell me where she was. All I've got is the phone number. I need the address so I can go get her or . . ."

"What is the number, sir?"

"Oh, it's 555–1097."

After a couple of seconds, the voice returned. "I'm sorry, sir, that number is unlisted and unpublished. I can't give you that information."

"But it could be an emergency. She sounded awful. I've heard her like this before. It's usually right before she has another breakdown."

Calmly, evenly, she said. "I'm sorry, sir. If it's an emergency, call 911. Have the police contact us. I need a court order before I can release this information."

"Okay, okay. I'll call 911. Thank you."

I replaced the phone. So it was a Fairfax County number. Sally Boszik could have two numbers to her home. No law against that. I checked my watch. Still enough time to call Ms. Boszik and rattle her cage before my noon meeting.

"Hello. Dr. Carleton's office."

"Sally Boszik, please."

"Speaking."

"Hello, Ms. Boszik, we have a mutual friend, Terry Onslow."

"I'm sorry, but I hardly know Terry Onslow. Who is this?"

"A friend, Sally. Terry's out of the picture now. You'll be dealing with me. But the deal is a little different. What say we get together to discuss it? How about tonight?"

Her "Fuck off, you creep," was punctuated with the crash of the receiver onto its cradle. The echo felt like a bayonet in the ear.

Sally Boszik didn't rattle easily. Round two would start tonight, say about eleven.

I stretched in the car and checked my watch. Ten of twelve.

I scanned the car's interior. Home, Sweet Home. I'd spent more time in this exoskeleton than I had anywhere else, even the motel room. I hadn't seen Sam in days, or talked to Randi, or seen a friend, or been home or to my office. I owned nothing but some clothes, a gun, and a car with a phone. This was not the life I thought I'd have. Not living in my car, by myself, at age forty. Of course, this is temporary, I told myself. I'll catch this shithead and it'll be over. Everything will go back to normal. Just the way it was. What if I don't catch this guy? How long do I do this?

My beeper went off. It was Kelly at the office. I called her back.

"Leo, it's the guy. I've got him on hold."

"Okay, connect me through and run the tape. When we're done, send it to Rocky to hold onto until I return to the office."

"Okay, Leo."

She made the connection and I spoke first.

"This is Leo Haggerty. Who am I talking to?"

"Don't fuck with me, asshole. You know who it is."

"No, I don't. Who is this?"

"Cut the shit. You've got something of mine and I want it back."

"I don't know what you're talking about."

"Jesus, that's lame. You ripped off that moron, Snipes. I want the key back, Haggerty. Now."

"I don't have it. Snipes is lying to you. He's still got it."

"Nice try, but I think not. Snipes knows better than to fuck with me. If I put the word out that he's ripped me off, there's no place he can hide. Besides, I know where he is. I'm getting tired of looking for you. So you give me back the key, and hey, we're even. You fuck this up for me and I will hunt you down. How long do you think you can keep hiding, you gutless cocksucker? What you gonna do? You gonna quit work? Sell your house? Leave town? Even if you do, you'll be looking over your shoulder the whole time. And I'll be there, and one day it'll happen. I won't do it like I did your buddy. I wasn't going to fuck with him. That was business. But you, you're pissing me off.

"How long do you think that honey of yours will stay put? She'll come by the house one day, because she left a dress there or something. And then I'm gonna have some serious fun with her. She's a stone fox, that bitch. So, what'll it be, Haggerty?"

"All right, all right. You win. I've got it. I mean, I don't have it but I know where it is. I can get it. I just need some time."

"Attaboy, Haggerty. I knew you had it. How much time do you need?"

"Uh, forty-eight hours. I can have it for you then. We'll set up an exchange. Whatever."

"Yeah, whatever. Okay. You've got forty-eight hours. I'll call you at nine, day after tomorrow. Don't fuck this up. I don't give anybody a second chance."

"No. I won't. I don't know what we were thinking of. I just want to give it back to you. Get this thing over with. You're right, I can't take this any longer."

"You know, Haggerty, Snipes was right about you."

"What do you mean?"

"He said your buddy was the balls of the outfit, but I could reason with you. I guess he was right. You got forty-eight hours."

Think what you want, shithead. Forty-eight hours is all you've got, too.

25

I picked up a jumbo 5-way and some garlic bread at Skyline and took them back to the motel. I punched on the TV and sat down at the desk to eat. The big story on all the local news was the mayor's arrest on a drug charge. And this only a day after he'd announced that he was winning the war on drug-related violence.

As usual, I speckled myself while I ate. Never could get that chili-coated spaghetti to behave. When I was done, I bagged all the debris and tossed it in the trashcan. Out came my address book for some more notes.

Was my mystery man a member of the Fourth Reich? His comments about Harold and the consequences of ripping him off led to that conclusion. If not them, then maybe another neo-Nazi group. Harold hadn't been entirely truthful with me. This was where I could use Arbaugh or Rhodasson's help. Take the description and put it into their computers, spit out a name and a history.

I closed up the notebook and emptied Reed's envelope. I tore off the first page of the printout and put the rest of it and one disk back into the envelope. On that sheet I wrote a concise narrative of everything I knew and addressed it to my lawyer, Walter O'Neil. In the event of my disappearance or death, he was to convey all the data to the police. I sealed up the envelope and set it aside. First thing tomorrow, I'd mail it to him.

My next step was to increase the pressure on Sally Boszik. But that wouldn't happen until later tonight.

I flipped the channel on the TV and watched a couple of music videos for the thinking-impaired, gave up, and turned it off.

My beeper went off and rescued me from myself. It was Sandy's number. I called back and got her on the line.

"Sandy, it's Leo. Did Sam just call me?"

"Yeah, hold on. Let me get her."

"Hello." Her voice was soft, the word tentative.

"Hello, Sam. I tried to reach you yesterday."

"I know. That's why I called."

"I'm glad you did. I miss you terribly."

"I miss you too, Leo."

"How are you doing?"

"Okay, I guess. I don't know. Mostly I sit and think. Sometimes I cry. Sometimes I'm numb."

My spectrum of emotion was enraged to numb. I didn't think she'd want to hear that.

"I spoke to that policeman again, Rhodasson."

"Oh, did he call you?"

"No. I don't think he knew where I was. I called him. I told him everything I told you in the hospital. He said it was helpful. They already have some leads. He's pretty sure they'll be able to find out who the guy is."

"I see. Well, that's good news."

"What's the matter, Leo? You don't sound like you think it's good news."

"No, it is. I guess I don't want to rely on the police, that's all."

"Why not, Leo? I'd think you'd want everybody possible on

this. The more people that are looking for this guy, the sooner we can stop this hiding, try to have a life again."

"You're right. I'm just not ready to turn everything over to the police. To rely on them for our safety. They fuck up. They make mistakes."

"And you don't?"

"No, of course I do. But it's just a job to them. It's our lives. I don't want to put that in anyone else's hands."

"Are you sure that's all it is, Leo?"

"What do you mean?"

"Don't treat me like a child, Leo. I know you. You mean to tell me that getting revenge isn't part of the reason you're pursuing this?"

"Do you have a problem with that?"

"Leo, that's not an answer to my question. If revenge is on your mind, don't use me to legitimize it. If I wanted him dead, I'd do it myself. You're doing this for you."

"Can you tell me that you don't want him dead?"

"No. Of course not. Do I want him dead? Yes. Every time I close my eyes and smell him on me, or feel him in me. Every time I have a cramp and remember that I'm empty inside. Yes, I want him dead. But would I do it? No. There's got to be a difference between him and me. I don't do that to people."

"Well, maybe I'm not different."

"Leo, that's not true."

"Oh, really? I've killed, what, three men already. What's one more?"

"Those were different, Leo. I know. I remember them. They were self-defense. You had no choice. That boy in the field. I remember how much that shook you up. The guy in the embassy. You saved that kid's life. And the guy in Virgin Gorda was trying to kill you. This is different, Leo. You want the violence. You're making it happen. You want the chance to kill this guy. You don't think it makes a difference? The man who killed that boy in the Lorton fields was sick about it. I don't think he'd be so keen to kill someone else. Borders crossed with impunity aren't borders anymore. You have to go further away each time before you'll stop yourself.

"I'm frightened, Leo. How far are you going to go this time? If you kill this man, what about next time? What will it take to trigger that response? You don't like how someone looks at you? Leo, please stop now, before you cross this border. It's different. You won't be the same as you were before.

"Leo, there are some things that once you do them, you can't undo them. You're never the same. I know. I felt that way about the baby. I'm different now. I wanted the baby, Leo. Our baby. I crossed the border. I wanted to be a mother. I was ready. Everything changed for me. I lost the baby but I didn't change back. I'm still a mother inside."

Somehow I'd lost my footing and wound up on my butt, sliding downhill straight toward a ravine. I opened my mouth as a brake but said nothing. I knew I was at some sort of crossroads with Sam. Every move I made, from going to work with Arnie, to staying away from the hospital, to this, had put me farther away from her. Whoever said that the tough times bring you together had eaten one too many smiley buttons. I knew I should agree with her. That was the way back. But was she right? What if she wasn't? How bad could that be? Was it worth putting more distance between us? I felt like we were on two ice floes, slowly breaking up and drifting apart. Soon it would be too far to jump from one to another and we'd be apart forever.

I wanted to jump. I really did. Instead, I just said, "Sam, let me think about what you've said. No matter what ultimately happens, I still need more information before I go to the police. I want to be able to hand him to them on a platter."

"What does that mean?"

"That means that I'm going to keep laying low. Keep trying to figure out what's going on and how to catch this guy. Just like I've been doing. I think that's the safest, best route for me and you."

"Okay, Leo. I've said my piece. Goodnight."

She hung up before I could reply.

No, I hadn't jumped. I'd dug my toes in, leaned way out and grabbed the other piece of ice with my fingers, and was holding them together for dear life. What a smart move.

26

I must have dozed off because the next thing I knew someone was pounding on the skin of the world. I looked around. No, just the door to my room.

I slid off the bed, walked over, and cracked the door. The manager was close enough to kiss. I just stared at her. We played dueling eyeballs for a while. She spoke first.

"Yeah, well, I just came by to tell you that you ain't paid for today. So I need the money or I'll have to ask you to leave."

I watched her talk. The words arrived an instant late, like a bad dubbing. She cocked her head, furrowed her brow, and put her hands on her hips.

"Did you hear me? I want my money, or you gotta go."

Everything synchronized. I smiled to reassure her that I was harmless and reached for my wallet. The fifty in her hand made her smile.

"You want it for two more days, then?"

I nodded. She tried to look past me to make sure she hadn't interrupted me making bombs or dismembering anyone. I didn't block her view.

"Okay, then. Thanks. Goodnight."

I closed the door and checked my watch. Time to go. I picked up the envelope from the desk and left.

On the way to Sally Boszik's I made two stops. First the post office and then a Burgerteria where I made a mistake and ordered their latest experimental sandwich. It tasted just like what it was: a pressed and shaped patty of assorted pork parts. Yummy.

Sally lived in a townhouse off Gallows Road. Fortunately, her block had only one exit. I took up my position at about 5:15 p.m. Sally showed up at a quarter to six.

She was a little past her prime, but not as far as me. She could still do nice things to a tight skirt and high heels, although she'd thickened a bit in the waist. Sometimes I think aging is a gravitational disorder. Things fall and then they stay there.

Her hair was streaked and wild. Her face plain and hard. Whatever hopes she once harbored there had been scrubbed off.

I pushed "Til Tuesday" into the tape player. Maybe when this was all over, Aimee Mann and I could compare notes. She did some amazing things with heartbreak.

Once Sally was inside the house, I gave her ten minutes to scan her mail, shuck her shoes, and make a drink. I dialed the number from the data disk and let it ring. Ten times and no reply. I waited fifteen minutes and tried again. Nothing.

I did that for two hours. All I had to show for it was a growing admiration for Sally Boszik's nerves and stamina. If it had been me, I'd have bolted a long time ago. Gone to a movie. Hid out in a mall until closing. No, she was still puttering around in there. Not even a nervous peek out the window.

Around eight, I decided to increase the pressure. Anxiety is the bastard offspring of unpredictability, so I started to vary the intervals between calls. Then the number of rings. Nothing. She hadn't even bothered to unplug the phone.

At ten-fifteen I set a C&P record for the most consecutive rings without reply not involving a birth announcement or a governor's pardon. Five. Ten. Fifteen. Twenty. Twenty-five. Thirty. Thirty-five. For . . . She picked it up. Silence. I waited for her to speak. She hung up. I rang back. One ring and she had it. This time, I spoke right away.

"I've been very patient with you, but you're going to have to . . ."

"You have a wrong number. Don't dial it again." Click.

I dialed back. Nothing. No ring. No connection. I dialed Sally Boszik's listed number. One ring, and she picked it up.

"Hello."

I said nothing.

"Hello. Anyone there? Goodbye, then."

I hung up. Mission accomplished. Connect Sally Boszik to the intruder's phone line. Worked like a charm. Except for one thing. The voices weren't the same.

27

Excitement fought exhaustion for possession of my remains and lost. I woke up clinging to the tattered remnants of a dream. I was an olive tree, twisted and gnarled, clinging to a hillside above an empty ruined city. I was ugly, but I was very old, and I was still there. The lofty cedars were all gone.

I stripped off the clothes I had slept in and took a stinging shower. Still dripping, I sat on the bed and called Ellen Moffatt at BMR. After we exchanged hellos, I asked her if she'd help me one more time.

"Depends on what it is."

"It's the same thing as before. I'm sure you've noticed that nobody has come around asking questions about the security rotation."

"True. So what do you want to know?"

"There's a phone number that I want checked. It's authorized to use your computer system. I want to know who got it authorized and how. It's assigned to Sally Boszik, but she doesn't know anything about it."

"That's it?"

"Yeah."

"Simple enough. I can go down and check the initial request log. It's part of my job anyway."

"So, it would have been part of Terry's, too?"

"Sure. We log in the requests for new authorizations and every once in a while we purge the list."

"How often?"

"Whenever somebody remembers to do it. This isn't the Federal Reserve Board or the Pentagon. Security here is in name only."

"How long will it take to find out?"

"As long as it takes to walk down and find the authorization request."

"Great. Here's the number to check. Call me back at this number." I gave her the number and my beeper number, hung up, and went to finish drying off.

I was almost finished dressing when she called back. I checked the beeper and dialed the number.

"Ellen?"

"Yes."

"What did you find out?"

"The request for the number came from Dr. Sylvia Francis. Sally was her secretary. She asked for it because Sally was going to be doing some work for her from her home, and this new number was unpublished. The notes say Sally had been getting some obscene calls so she'd changed her number. That do it?"

"When did she file this request?"

"About four months ago."

"One last thing. What does Sylvia Francis look like?"

"She's short, five feet two maybe. A little on the heavy side. Blond hair, page-boy style. Wears glasses. She should have been a nun, if you ask me."

"Why do you say that?"

"She never smiles. She always looks disappointed. Life never turns out the way she wants it to."

"Why a nun, then?"

"I don't know. I guess if this life isn't good enough for you, you should try the next one. How can God disappoint you? He's perfect, right?"

"For some people even that isn't good enough."

"Well, Sylvia Francis is one of them, then. If she ever wins the Nobel Prize, as she thinks she should, she'll bitch about how it doesn't go with what she's wearing."

"Well, thanks again. You've been a big help."

"Thank you for not blowing the whistle on us."

I hung up and called my stockbroker.

"Mr. Davis's office, how may I help you?"

"Warwick Davis, please. Leo Haggerty calling."

"Hold, please. I'll see if he's available."

His secretary switched lines and Wick said hello. His voice was as soft as a cat's step.

"Hello, Wick. I need some information."

"Regarding?"

"A possible investment. Palmetto Research Company. They're an R&D firm over here in Tysons. Pharmaceuticals, biogenetics. That sort of stuff."

"Isn't that rather speculative for you, Leo?"

"What the hell. I need to loosen up a bit. I just got a nice bonus from the boss. I figure I can play with a little bit of it."

"Do you know what they're trading as?"

"Nope. Don't know anything about them."

"Why the interest, then?" Warwick registered the unusual like a seismograph. He was convinced that fortunes were made and lost in the space between the tremor and the quake.

"Rumor has it they're on the verge of a major medical breakthrough."

"I see. Well, hold on a second. Let me see where they're trading."

I descended into the eighth ring of Muzak and served my time with the synthesizer version of that investment house anthem, "Born in the USA."

"I'm sorry, Leo. I don't find them being traded on any of the markets. Are you sure they're a public company?"

"I'm not sure of anything, Wick. Can you find out something about them for me? I think this is going to be a hot area for investing, and if they're on the forefront, I'd like a piece of the action."

"I'll look into it. It might take some time to track them down. They may have a prospectus out but haven't been approved for public trading yet."

"Thanks. Any idea how long it'll take?"

"I should have something for you before the close of day."

"Great. I'll be out of the office today, so let me give you my beeper number. Let me know as soon as you have anything and I'll call you right back."

"I'll be in touch."

I called Information and got addresses and phone numbers for Palmetto Research Corporation and Sylvia Francis.

I called the office and Kelly told me that the service had been calling since 9:00 a.m. I called back and asked for my messages.

"Just one, Mr. Haggerty. A Reverend Brown. He calls every hour on the hour. Has since midnight. He's quite upset that you haven't called in. He hasn't left a message. Just wants to know if you've called in."

"Sorry. When he calls in, tell him I checked in. Tell him I'm okay and that Wardell should untie the Pfeiffers. They could drown. He'll know what it means."

"Yes, sir."

I put down the phone and said, "Shit." It was a stupid thing to forget. I needed to feel that I was getting this mess under control and there was no way I could cite this as evidence.

When I called Kelly back, she told me that Arnie's ashes were in my office. They didn't know where else to put them.

"Thanks, Kelly. Just leave them there. And tell Frank not to touch them. He gets nervous when he can't straighten something up. If you don't watch him, he'll throw them out."

"I'll watch him."

"Any other messages?"

"That lieutenant called again. He still wants to talk to you."

"I'll call him again. How're things going?"

"Okay, I guess. Everybody's real tense around here."

"That's just 'cause Frank's such an anal retentive."

"No. That's part of it. But you've been out almost a week. Everyone knows you're in trouble. They know about Arnie Kendall and Sam. I think they're worried about you."

"Well, tell them it's getting sorted out. I should be back in the next few days."

"They wanted me to tell you that if you need anything, to call them on their beepers, any time, day or night."

"Thanks, Kelly. Tell them that if I need anything, I'll call. Honest."

"All right. Be careful, then."

I left the motel and had lunch at Anita's over in Vienna. New Mexicans pride themselves on having the hottest peppers in North America. I doubted that once and wound up pouring beer all over my dinner in a little Taos taqueria while I tried to put out my face. I respectfully avoided any dishes Anita marked with flames and settled for a chimichanga and a beer.

In the car I called Lieutenant Arbaugh and left a message and the office number. Another round of telephone tag, pursued in good faith or its appearance, and frustrated by our respective good fortune to be busy, busy men.

In the next twenty-four hours I needed to tie Sylvia Francis incontrovertibly to the break-in and damage to BMR's data. With that, I could squeeze the name of her associate out of her and wrap this up. If that didn't happen, he and I would meet and settle it our own way, whatever that meant. One way or the other, it would soon be over.

My beeper went off. It was Wick Davis. While his secretary went to get him, I drummed the steering wheel.

"Leo, your request turned out to be quite interesting. Had to do a little detective work on this one."

"And you found?"

"A little history first. Palmetto Research Corporation is an 8A company."

I resisted the impulse to go "Hunh" and let him proceed.

"That means it's minority-owned. The owner is a black

woman named Fanny Shoate. Now as an 8A company she gets special treatment on bids for government work. These special conditions hold for a limited period of time. The idea is that these minority companies will become competitive, and as they are phased out of governmental bids they will win contracts on their own."

"And if they don't?"

"Then they've had the free lunch, so to speak, and then they go out of business. It's a laudable plan and for some entrepreneurs it's a godsend. They get their chance to make good, and they leave the program able to compete with other companies on an equal footing. However, like all laudable plans, this one can be corrupted. You can put up a figurehead minority owner, plunder the government contracts for years, siphon off enormous amounts of cash, go belly up, and retire rich. There's no penalty if you don't succeed. All you need is a good accountant to dazzle the procurement investigators. It's just like drugs only without the bullets."

"Is that what Palmetto is?"

"It's not clear what Palmetto is. It's a pharmaceutical research and development firm and they're near the end of their 8A status.

"A few months ago they issued a prospectus to investors. Looks like they intended to trade as a public company. Now, at that time they had to disclose their assets and so on. All of their contracts were government ones and were nearly completed. They did claim to be starting a new AIDS project and were trying to generate the operating capital by selling shares of stock. Here's where it gets interesting, and by the way, Leo, next time you want me to do some legwork for you, just ask. Don't feed me this eager-investor nonsense. It insults my intelligence and robs me of some fun. I love a good mystery, too, you know."

"I'm sorry, Wick. I know you're busy. I didn't think you'd do it if it wasn't business."

"Oh, it is business, Leo. I could just as easily bill you for a consultation instead of collecting a commission for a sale. But this is fun for me, so there's no charge."

"Thanks, Wick. It won't happen again." He'd graciously downplayed the point. I'm glad I'm not a friend of mine. I couldn't afford it.

"Well, anyway, the prospectus was withdrawn a few weeks ago. No reason given, just withdrawn."

"Do you have any ideas?"

"Well, there's a couple of likely reasons. One, a private buyer has approached them. Some sort of takeover or buyout. If one of their competitors has the money, it may be prudent to absorb them now for a set price rather than lose a portion of the market to them from now on, or have to do it later for more money.

"A second reason would be that the company is having problems with its new project, or that the market in general has bottomed out for its product. There was no investor interest, so they withdrew the prospectus."

"How do you read it, Wick?"

"The biomedical field is very unstable these days. The FDA scandal with the generics has spooked a lot of people. They're worried about lawsuits consuming profits. This is not a good time for a small firm with shaky or nonexistent capital to try to interest investors. AIDS research is even trickier, even though that's where the profit potential is greatest right now. There's a tug-of-war over the way research is being conducted that makes this a terribly volatile and unpredictable area."

"Who's doing the tugging?"

"On one hand, there's the activists who want government procedures and requirements changed so that drugs can be made more quickly available to people with AIDS. They want the FDA to tolerate the idea of human guinea pigs if it'll accelerate the discovery of an effective treatment or vaccine.

"On the other side is the FDA, which is concerned about releasing medications that do nothing or are lethal to people. They don't want to give up control of the safety and efficacy of drugs."

"How does all this affect the drug companies?"

"The result for the drug companies is rapidly changing performance criteria for FDA approval into the market. Who's closer to a breakthrough is always changing because the rules are always changing. On top of that, the potential rewards are now even greater."

"I don't follow."

"As the FDA gives up control and lets medications into the market more easily, they lose their control over pricing. In the past, they could say that without a price cap of X dollars per unit, there was no approval. Now, with drugs being released that are essentially still in the investigatory phase, they don't know what's going to turn out to be effective. Drugs are being tested in the market, not before. A price cap after approval is like closing the barn door after the horse has bolted. Whoever gets out there first with anything that's at all effective and less awful than the disease can make a fortune."

"So the bottom line is that AIDS victims may get a drug that helps them sooner than before, but they might not be able to pay for it?"

"You got it, Leo."

28

I drove over to Palmetto Research Corporation. They had the twelfth floor in a large office building. I found a space where I could watch the front door of the building and backed into it. I checked my tank. Almost full. Then I called Kelly.

"I need some help on a surveillance. Who's in the office?"

"Burdette's here, finishing a report." Burdette was less than no help. He was the worst driver I'd ever seen. He thought you lined up the dotted lines with your hood ornament.

"I'm in Tysons. Anybody live out here that I can call?"

"Let me check. Hold on . . . Del Winslow lives near you. Here's his number."

Del was a hardworking guy of modest talents. His mother must have had footlights in mind when she named him Delmarva, after the eastern shore peninsula. So far he was more Del than Marva-lous, but he could execute a two-man tail.

Fortunately he was home when I called and he drove into the lot ten minutes later. He sauntered over and I rolled down the window.

Del was six feet two, maybe 140 pounds, capped off with a diamond stud in his ear, sidewalls, and a flat top. He wore two-toned shoes, pleated chocolate slacks, and a pink shirt.

"Mr. Haggerty, what's happening?"

"We're happening, Del. I'm going to make a call to someone in there and hopefully annoy her enough to come running out, jump in her car, and lead me to someone I very much want to meet."

"This 'her,' what's she look like?"

"Short. A bit heavy. Blond hair, page-boy, glasses. A look on her face like someone spit in her soup."

"Car?"

"Don't know."

"How do you want to handle it?"

"I'll be lead car. You follow. Consider it a hot tail. If she does anything funny—last-minute turns, a sudden park job, U-turns, whatever—I'll break off and go parallel for a couple of blocks. Then fall in behind you. I don't want to lose this lady."

"What if she spots us and hightails it? Any hot pursuit?"

"Down, Del. If we're blown, she won't go anywhere near the person I'm looking for. If we're spotted, just call it off and go home. Beside, hot pursuit is from La-La Land. We miss her today, we come back tomorrow. We get them with patience, not firepower."

"You know, Mr. Haggerty, this p.i. business is not what I thought it would be."

"You disappointed?"

"I guess so."

"Don't be. Nothing's as good as it's cracked up to be. Except sex. Sometimes."

"That's not real encouraging. I was going to make a career of this. Delmarva Winslow, the famous shamus."

"You know the Pinkerton symbol, Del?"

"Yeah, the Eye. Ever vigilant. It sees all, knows all."

"Right. Well, the eye that sees all also sees what it doesn't like and stays open anyway."

Del looked puzzled, like my dog when as a boy I gave her a

command like "Roll over, lie down, sit, paw, stay." She was sure that I didn't mean that string of non sequiturs, and that I'd soon realize it and do the right thing, like get a biscuit.

"Sure, Mr. Haggerty, whatever. I was just asking if we could do a little hot pursuit." Del walked back to his car, looked over his shoulder at me, and shook his head.

Once Del was ready, I called Palmetto Research Corporation.

"Good afternoon. Palmetto Research."

"Sylvia Francis, please."

"Hold."

Ten seconds later I met Dr. Sylvia Francis.

"Yes."

"Hello, Dr. Francis, my name is Arbaugh. I'm a detective with the County Police. I wonder if I might meet with you today?"

Nothing.

"Uh, Dr. Francis, are you there?"

"Yes, I'm here. I was just, uh, checking my calendar. May I ask what this is in reference to?"

"We're looking into the disappearance of Terence Onslow. He worked at Biomedical Research. I understand you were previously employed there. Let me see here," I paused as if perusing some notes, "yes, you both worked on the same project, Dr. Schatzkin's study. You were an investigator and he worked in the computer section. Is that right?"

"Yes, Lieutenant. That's right."

"So you knew Mr. Onslow?"

"Yes, but only slightly. He came on just before I left. I really can't imagine what I could tell you."

"Let me be the judge of that. People know a lot more than they think. It's just a matter of asking the right questions."

"Can we do this by phone? I'm quite busy. I've got research of my own to attend to."

"No. I'm sorry, I have to do this in person. By the way, what kind of research are you involved in?"

"Is that important, Lieutenant?"

"I have no idea, Doctor. Seems to me you can't tell whether something is important until after you know what it is. How it squares with everything else you know. Isn't research like that? You collect all the data, but you don't know what it means until it's all in?"

"Yes, that's true. To answer your question, I'm studying a variety of drug combinations to see if we can block the transmission of the AIDS virus to the fetus of infected mothers. Some of the drugs that are available now may not be effective after exposure to the virus or after the infection appears but may block the initial invasion of the virus genes into host cells. Does that help you, detective?"

"Like I said, I don't know. I'm just a researcher, like you. What you're describing sounds real important, though. If you found some combination that worked, you'd have a vaccine, wouldn't you?"

"Technically, no. We'd have a preventive treatment for a portion of the population at risk, the children of infected mothers. From there we'd have a much better sense of how to go about creating a vaccine."

"Good luck, sounds like there's a Nobel Prize in there somewhere. I appreciate how valuable your time is, but do you think we might be able to meet sometime today?"

"I'm sorry. That's really not possible. I'm in the lab all day today."

"Okay. How about tomorrow? You pick the time. I'll work around your schedule."

"Tomorrow's not good either. Really. Are you sure this is necessary?"

"I'm afraid it is. If tomorrow's not good, just tell me when. I'm at your disposal."

"Oh, all right. How long will it take?"

"I don't know. Thirty minutes, maybe a little longer."

"Okay, how about five o'clock today, after the lab staff goes home?"

"Thank you, Doctor. I'll be at your office at five. You might want to jot down some notes. Anything you can remember about Onslow. I find that helps me organize my thoughts. Might speed up the interview."

"I don't think that'll be necessary. I can't even remember what he looked like."

"Funny you should say that. That's what everyone says about him. A harmless little guy. Wouldn't hurt a fly."

"Yes. Goodbye, Lieutenant."

"Goodbye, Doctor."

I hung up and checked my watch.

She was pretty nervy. I hoped that I'd gotten under her skin enough to make her contact her partner and find out how deep a hole she was in.

Ten minutes and forty-eight seconds later she came striding out of the building. She slid into a blue-gray Mercedes coupe, slammed the door, gunned the engine, and sped off out of the lot. She was under a lot of stress and I knew for a fact that she hadn't slept well last night.

29

I followed her car as it slalomed down the hill, across Leesburg Pike, and then toward Old Courthouse Road. She wasn't concerned about being tailed. I hoped she was angry and better yet, scared stupid. At Chain Bridge Road, she slewed right as the light went from yellow to red. I followed less dramatically. We headed into Vienna. I picked up the phone and called Del.

"Yeah?"

"I want you to pass her, Del, but don't get into the same lane. Keep her in your rear-view mirror. We're heading into Vienna and it's a traffic light every hundred feet. The way she's driving, I'd have to be in her trunk to make every light. If she turns off Maple, stop in the next block, call me, and tell me which way she went."

"I'm on it." With that, he sped past me. I half expected to hear a hearty high-ho silver.

We flew past the residential areas, but she began to slow down as we approached the commercial strip through the heart of town. Fortunately, getting pulled over for speeding was not on the agenda. We crawled through town from light to light. Past Beulah Road, then Park Street, which bisects the town. At Nutley, she turned left. Off to the races, I figured. I-66 was two miles away. Instead, she turned right on Courthouse and then left into Nottaway Park. I followed down the winding entrance to the parking lot. After ramming the Mercedes into a slot, she jumped out and slammed the door. She stalked off, pounding her steps like she had an enemy lashed to each shoe. I found a spot and backed in. I watched her march off toward the pavilion in the woods. Del pulled into the lot, drove past me, and backed into a spot. I zipped up my coat, reached into the back seat for a hat, and found my Falls Church Flatliners Cap. It's a group dedicated to the belief that any activity above the brain stem is hazardous to your health. We got together to eat beef jerky and corn nuts and one-up each other with obscure books and films. The ones waiting to vault into cult status, but now sitting in the anteroom of the merely notorious.

I slipped on a pair of non-corrective glasses, got out of the car, and sauntered over to Del. He rolled down his window.

"What now?"

"You got a ball with you?"

"Sure, the trunk's full of them. What do you want?"

"How about a Frisbee?"

"Yeah, why?"

"We're going to play fetch. C'mon, let's go."

Del uncoiled from the car, opened his trunk, and handed me the Frisbee.

"Let's go over to the open field there. We'll start close together and just play catch. Start to back up a little bit at a time and when we're far enough apart, I want you to wing one into the woods. Try to get it near the pavilion."

"So I toss it and you fetch."

"See, isn't being a detective exciting work?"

"Be still, my beating heart."

"Before we do this, why don't you take off your tie, roll up your sleeves, try to look a little more casual?"

"No sweat."

Del and I wandered over to the grassy area, casually tossing the Frisbee back and forth. Every once in a while I turned so I could get a look at Sylvia. She was seated at a picnic table under the pavilion. Her legs were crossed and her angry foot kicked an invisible enemy.

A few minutes passed and Del and I were now far enough apart for an innocent overthrow. He wound up and sent one skimming high over my head.

As I loped after it, he called out, "Sorry about that."

The Frisbee was in the underbrush off to the left of the pavilion. Out of the corner of my eye I saw a second figure at the table. I unzipped my jacket and shrugged my holster forward a bit.

I bent down to pick up the Frisbee and turned casually toward the table. Sylvia Francis was pacing back and forth, arms held tight across her chest. She spoke in a ferocious whisper. I couldn't make out the words, but the tone of rancid contempt was unmistakable. Her target was a middle-aged black woman with short gray hair. Silently absorbing the rage, her shoulders sagged and she wrung her hands in distress. Her head kept bobbing up and down, the bitter yes of a chronic victim when a long-overdue cruelty has finally arrived. Sylvia Francis was telling her partner just how far up a certain creek they both were and just how far away the nearest paddle was.

30

I strolled back to Del and pretended to show him a defect in the Frisbee.

"Let's move back to our cars. This isn't the meeting I was hoping for. We'll pick up the surveillance when she leaves," I said.

We ambled down the slight decline and passed through the notched log fence. At Del's car, we leaned against the body and chatted about the Redskins. Every once in a while I scanned the woods and confirmed that the two women were still there. Francis continued her pacing, interspersed with what I guessed were palms-up pleadings to the other to understand the enormity of their predicament. Most of these were addressed to the top of her head as she slumped in her seat.

I was pretty sure the other woman was Fanny Shoate, the head of Palmetto Research. Next order of business was proving it.

When Francis stormed out of the woods, I went to my car and timed my ignition and departure with hers.

We moved briskly but not wildly through Vienna. From Nutley, she turned left onto Tapawingo and followed it over to Park. There she went left on Cedar, then left on Labbe Lane. I lived three blocks away.

I followed her past her house and pulled in four doors down. Once she was inside her house, I called Del, who was idling on Cedar Lane.

"She's home. I want someone to sit on her all night. I'll start. Why don't you come back, say around eleven, and we'll switch off."

"Sure. You gonna watch her from there?"

"No, I'm too conspicuous. It's a dead-end street so we can use one of the nearby office lots."

I pulled out of my spot and cruised up to the main street. A three-story office building to the left had a lot with a clear view of her house. I drove into it, found a spot I liked, and cut the engine. Del pulled in alongside me.

"Anything you want before I go home?" he asked.

"Yeah. Here's a ten. There's a Seven-Eleven up the street. Get me a large coffee and two of their biggest sandwiches. I don't care what they are."

"Be right back."

When Del returned with dinner, I took it through the window and put it on the seat next to me. Then I eased back my seat so I could stretch out some.

At five o'clock, Francis still hadn't left for her meeting with Arbaugh. I called her office, identified myself as Arbaugh, and asked for her. Her secretary told me that she had taken ill and gone home early. I left a message that I would call again tomorrow. I left a message with Kelly and Wick Davis to get me a description of Fanny Shoate.

Four hours later, I was in Flatliner heaven. Barely awake, with just enough juice from my crocodile brain to keep my lids up and register any major changes in the world. Only the bare essentials. Nothing gaudy like a thought.

My dashboard clock read 10:15 when she came out the front door with a bag in each hand. She set them down at the curb and hurried back inside. Two green plastic garbage bags. I eyed them as eagerly as a kid finding Santa's sack unattended. Ah, garbage, sweet garbage. I was rapturous. What possibilities in those Hefty Cinch-Sacks. One last chance to yoke Francis to Onslow and to her mercenary. One last chance at a piece of hard evidence to complete the circuit. To light up Dr. Sylvia Francis. If there were riches in that muck, I would have some control over tomorrow's events. If not, then I'd make the best of them I could, but with drastically curtailed options.

I couldn't wait any longer. Not with those treasures out on the sidewalk. Suppose she decided there was something valuable in there and came out to reclaim them. I called Del.

"Hello. Del, this is Haggerty. Get over here. Right now. Immediately. I don't care if you're buck naked."

"All right, all right. I'll be there in five minutes."

"Make it three. I'll pay the ticket."

When Del pulled up next to me, I told him to go to the 7-Eleven and buy some large green trashbags and enough newspapers to scrunch up and fill them.

Del returned with the stuff, put it into my car, and hopped in. While we filled up the bags, I talked.

"Now listen. We're going to go down there and switch these bags for her trash. Her house has the copper siding on the top of the front porch. I'm leaving as soon as I've got the trash. You're on her until I return in the morning. If she goes anywhere or has any visitors, call me on my beeper, immediately. No matter what the time is." I started the engine. "Del, one last thing. Don't lose her. I don't care if you get burned. Just don't lose her. I want to know where she is at all times. There's no case to protect here. It all goes down tomorrow. You understand?"

"Have no fear, Delmarva's here."

I rolled down my window as we backed out of the lot and headed for her house. As we rolled slowly down the block, I listened for any dogs. Sweet silence. We rolled past her house and turned in the cul-de-sac at the end.

As we headed back, Del asked, "Is this legal, what we're doing?"

"Absolutely. The laws of garbage are all with us. It's out for pickup, in an open area and unlocked. That makes it public domain. Slide out with the bags. Put them on the curb and toss hers in the car. If I have to leave anything behind, it'll be you, not the trash."

"I hear you."

I stopped in front of her bags. Del ghosted out, dropped the matching bags, put hers in the car, and pulled the door closed behind him.

"All right. Well done. You're now a professional garbologist."

Del looked thrilled. I laughed. "Never saw this on TV, did you? Well, this is real detective work, Del. This is nothing, though. Next, we'll do a motel dumpster. Say in August, when the smell's so bad it'll make your nose bleed. And the flies and bees are all over your head while you fish out the bags with a coathanger. Then it's rubber gloves and tetanus-shot time. You come across some strange shit going through other people's garbage."

I dropped him at his car and headed back to the motel. I felt like my birthday and Christmas had arrived. If I'd had anyone to share it with, I might even have been happy.

31

I carried the bags into my room and set them on the floor by the bed. Returning to the car, I took a plastic tarpaulin and latex gloves from the trunk.

Back in the room, I turned on all the lights and unfolded the tarpaulin so that it covered the bed. Years ago, the latex gloves were mostly for protection from the distasteful or disgusting. Nowadays, even an accidental contact with a stranger's bodily fluids was fraught with danger. I pushed the fingers down and flexed my hands. All I needed was a hunchbacked dwarf as an assistant and a raging storm outside. So, Doctor, I mused, what wonders will spring from this detritus?

The first bag had two smaller plastic bags inside. I pulled them out, set one on the floor, and dumped the other on a corner of the tarpaulin. My experienced eye concluded "Basic Bathroom" before it all stopped moving. I picked through ripped panty hose, moist Kleenex, a disposable razor, cotton balls with makeup on them, soap slivers, Q-Tips, a toilet paper roller, a burned-out bulb, and a couple of tampon tubes.

Once these were rebagged, I emptied the second bag. This was from her laundry room. Dryer lint, an old sponge, cleaning rags, an empty Clorox jug, and an Arm & Hammer detergent box.

I sealed up the two little bags in the larger green bag. Slivers of doubt started to push through me. Maybe there'd be nothing here. Maybe she had a shredder in her house. Maybe she was real careful, too.

This bag had a smaller one inside. I set that out and dumped the larger one onto the center of the bed. This was "Classic Kitchen." I spread it out evenly and stepped back. Maybe I should spray a fixative on it and call it art: *Suburban Spill-life*. Maybe not.

I started picking my way through coffee filters and grounds, an empty fifth of Jack Daniel's, Diet Coke cans, junk mail addressed to resident, crumpled napkins, and balled-up aluminum foil that I opened up to no avail.

Next were a soapless steel wool pad, paper towels, an egg box, the wrapper to a stick of butter, and a carry-out menu from a local Chinese place. The only food was two grapefruit rinds and a steak bone. Food disposers have added years to a garbologist's career. No molds, fungi, or larvae anchoring themselves to your gloves or crawling up your arms.

The rest of the pile was tea bags, corks, a cereal box, a bag of frozen peas, two Mexican TV-dinner packages, and an empty salsa jar.

The last bag was almost all mail. Probably the trashcan in her home office. I spread all the papers out and read each one carefully before tossing it back in the bag. First to go was her professional mail. Book clubs, workshop announcements, association meetings. Then I discarded her magazines, grocery tabs, late notices on her car loan and mortgage, and the agenda for a homeowners' meeting. There was no personal correspondence in the pile. The last papers were bills. Some were just envelopes. Some had the stubs with them. Mobil, Exxon, Virginia Power, Falls Church Water Authority, Skyline Health Club, Media General Cable, Bloomingdale's, Macy's, AAA Trash Removal, Dr. Harry Joyce M.D., Obstetrics and Gynecology. Not a thing of use on any of them. Ripped up credit card chits told no tales. I flipped over the next bill. C&P. The long-distance call log was not there, only the pages explaining how the bill was computed and what taxes were levied. However, across the top of each page were printed the user's phone numbers. There was Sylvia Francis's name on the account and the back door she had used into BMR's data banks. The circle was completed, and when it closed I heard the click of handcuffs.

32

Riding my optimism, I packed up my few belongings. I wanted to remove any trace that I'd ever lived like this. That done, I took a shower and called my service.

"Hello, this is Leo Haggerty. I have a message for Reverend Brown. Tell him that I'm fine and I believe this will be my last night under a rock. If things go well, it should all be over tomorrow and I'll call to confirm that. Do you have that?"

"Yes, Mr. Haggerty. Is that all?"

"Yes . . . uh, no. I have a message for Randi Benson. 'Hang in there. I'm sorry this all happened. It'll be over soon. Love, Leo.' Thanks."

"You're welcome."

I lay down on the bed and played out all the options I could imagine. How to approach Sylvia Francis. How she might react. What my response should be. I tried to anticipate all her qualms, imagine her conflicts, her needs and fears, and how they balanced. How to shunt her into doing what I wanted and to think that it was also best for her. When I was done, I saw a way to let her maze be my funnel. Her shrewd negotiations my inevitability.

Tomorrow, our dreams would clash and then we'd pick our way through the debris we call life.

I called a friend and made some arrangements for the day's events. Like Mr. Rickey said, "Luck is the residue of preparation."

My last call was to Sam. Mercifully, she answered the phone herself.

I sat in silence for a while, then asked, "Why is this so hard?"

"A lot's happened, Leo. It's happened to us alone. None of it's easy to talk about, especially on the phone."

"Can't we try? It's not going to be like this forever. A day, two at the most, and it'll be all over. We can go home and start living again."

"Leo, it's not going to be over. Not for a long time. Not for me, anyway."

"You're right. I'm sorry. Is there anything I can do for you? Any way I can help? There isn't anything I wouldn't do for you."

"No, Leo, stop. Please don't say that." There was a steel edge to her plea. The executioner asks the condemned to have some dignity.

I said nothing.

"Leo."

"Yes, I'm here."

"You can do one thing for me. Tell me the truth. Why is this man after you? What did you do? Why did this happen to us, to you, to me."

The lie was on my tongue instantly, but the truth was paralytic. I knew what I should do, but that wasn't enough. Insight isn't all it's cracked up to be. It'll name your crossroads, but it won't move your tongue.

I scribbled a few quick equations on the walls of my skull. What does she know? Guess? Wish? Fear? Which way is out? What can I keep? What gets left behind?

I opened my mouth and a stranger said, "The night I was out with Arnie, the guy we picked up planted a key in Arnie's car. That's what the guy wants. That's what it's all about."

"Thank you, Leo. That's pretty much what I thought."

I sat there in a silence I rarely ever knew. No plots, no deeds, no plans played in my head. No voices, no images, no future. Just the empty present. The slowing click of an empty movie reel.

"What are you going to do, Leo?"

"I don't know."

"Let the police handle it, Leo. If you have anything, give it to them. Let them bring him in. You won't fix anything by killing him. Arnie won't come back. I won't feel any different. What's important happened between you and me, not him."

From the frozen center of things, I said, "Maybe I'll feel better. Maybe it'll fix that."

"And maybe you won't, Leo. This guy killed Arnie. What makes you think you can take him? Did you ever think of that?"

"All the time, Sam. All the time."

"Then keep thinking, Leo. You haven't made one right move in this yet."

33

At five, I woke up, showered, dressed, and called Del.

"Hello."

"Good morning, Del. How's sleeping beauty?"

"Just that. Lights out at eleven forty-five. Been that way ever since."

"Excellent. I'm on my way over. What do you want for breakfast?"

"Where you going?"

"Don't you get your hopes up. It'll be styrofood no matter where I get it."

"Okay. How about a biscuit and gravy and coffee?"

"Coming up. I should be there about six-fifteen."

I cleared my stuff out of the room, turned in the key at the office, and drove away. One more day and I'd have been out of clothes.

When I pulled up next to Del, he shot me a quick look and smiled when I showed him our treats. He unlocked his car and I slid in and handed him his breakfast in a bag.

We unpacked and set out our coffees. I checked my egg, sausage, hash brown sandwich for symmetry and worked my mouth around its perfect preformed circularity. Del handed me his notes from the surveillance. After setting out her trash,

Sylvia Francis had stayed downstairs for about thirty minutes. Lights out at 11:07. Upstairs, lights on until 11:45. Probably showering or a little reading. All quiet after that. No lights. No visitors. Nothing.

"Anybody notice that you were here?" I asked and worked on the sandwich.

"No. The only foot traffic was a guy walking his dog, about ten-fifty. I could see him but he didn't get up this far. At the end of the block he turned around and headed back. He did let his retriever do a nasty all over his neighbor's lawn, and he didn't clean it up."

"High crimes in suburbia, Del. What can I say?" Wiping my mouth, I hastened breakfast on with some caffeinated corrosive.

"Couple of teenagers came in late, around one. Also had some company here in the lot."

"Yes?"

"Couple of kids making out. So I rolled down my window, hit the stereo, and they vanished."

"Any police around?"

"Couple of times. Down Cedar Lane. I slid down when they came by. They didn't see me. Two cruisers were in the Mobil over there about three, swapping donuts and bullshit. That's about it."

When Del finished eating, I said, "Let's go down to her house. Park as close as you can. I'm going to go calling on our subject."

Del backed out, turned around in the lot, and drove down the street. He parked three spots up from Sylvia Francis's front door.

I slid out, and before I slammed the door, I ducked down and told Del, "If I'm not out in thirty minutes, call the cops."

Del checked his watch and nodded.

I pushed the doorbell and put my thumb over the peephole. Two more rings and I was rewarded with a "Who is it?"

"Courier, ma'am."

"It's awfully early for a delivery."

"Well, it's marked extremely urgent, and we guarantee round-the-clock service. That's why we're Early Bird Courier."

"All right, step back where I can see you."

I did as she asked. When the door opened, I congratulated myself for keeping the windbreaker with the name tag and the billed cap in the trunk. Add a clipboard, an empty manila envelope, and a smile, and presto, you're ubiquitous and benign.

Sylvia Francis stepped from behind the door. One hand gripped her china blue silk robe at the throat, the other demanded her package.

I stepped forward and handed her the clipboard to sign. She reached for it with both hands. I poked it against her chest, surged into her house, and closed the door behind me. She staggered back. Before she could turn and run, I pulled out my gun and got her full attention.

"Oh my God." She gasped and backed away haltingly.

"Not quite. But thanks, anyway."

"What do you want?" she asked and then gripped her robe tighter, as if that held the answer.

It never ceases to amaze me how precious words are when our lives are at stake. We seem to believe that if we're still talking, composing thoughts, exchanging them, reasoning together, then we can't possibly be screaming and bleeding. As if thinking and dying were mutually exclusive. Gunpoint conversations do have the purity of distilled desperation, though.

"I just want to talk to you," I drawled and punctuated that thought with a big grin.

"Okay, sure, we can talk. Whatever." Sylvia relaxed and nodded her head enthusiastically. Her eagerness to talk reflected her confidence in her mind. She'd lull me with her patience and interest in whatever I had to say, but her cunning mind would plan a trap for me. If we were going to match wits, then she was in no danger from me.

"Good. You see, I tried to talk to you once before, but you

didn't have any time for me. So here I have to go and do something like this."

"I'm sorry, really. I don't remember the situation. I'm sure there was a good reason why we couldn't talk then."

"Oh, there was." I pointed my gun at her sofa. "Why don't we sit and relax. No need to be so tense."

"Sure, uh, can I get you some coffee or something?" Her hands trembled as she made the offer.

"Is it fresh? I just can't stand instant."

"Yes, I was just putting it on. Uh, are you hungry? I've got some fresh croissants." I furrowed my brow. "Uh, rolls."

"Sure, yeah, that's good. Some of them." I wasn't sure how long I could keep this up, but it was fun.

I followed her into the kitchen. She pushed a button on a small drip coffee maker and opened a bakery bag. While she did that, I reached down and unplugged her kitchen phone. Then I sat down and crossed my legs and let my gun dangle as casually as a cigarette.

I watched her back as she moved barefoot from cupboard to cupboard, getting cups, plates, spoons. A memory of Sam, padding about, sun dappling her legs under one of my shirts, shuddered through me and I almost shot her on the spot.

She microwaved the croissants, put them on two plates, poured the coffee, and looked up between each action to see if I was still smiling. I lifted my cup and beamed at her, letting her know I relished her every act of service.

"Would you like some butter or jam on that?"

"Yeah, that sounds good. And how about some cream for this coffee?"

She brought the items from the refrigerator, set them out on the table, and sat down with her hands in her lap. I put down my coffee and pointed my gun right between her eyes.

"Take out the knife you put in your pocket and put it on the table. Slowly."

She clenched her jaw and slowly reached into the robe. The blade she put on the table was six inches of carbon steel.

"A little much for spreading butter, don't you think?"

I pulled the blade over and balanced it on my saucer.

Sylvia's blond hair was wet and slicked back, not a good look for her. Her ears were long-lobed, thin and translucent, like natural pearls mounted on her head.

"So, let's talk," I began affably. "I called you at your office to discuss your relationship with Mr. Terry Onslow, and you didn't want to talk. Now I can understand your reluctance. This could be a trap. I could be bluffing. You already had a deal going to get your data back from Onslow." That last nugget got her attention.

"I don't have time to screw around with you, so I'm going to prove to you that you have to deal with me. Here's the bottom line. Terry Onslow found out that you were backdooring your way into BMR's data base and fucking around with their data. So he deleted the real data and hid it from you. You need that stuff pretty bad, so you hired somebody to get it back. Well, your boy fucked up. I've got the data. So you have to deal with me."

"That's all very interesting, Mr. . . . ."

"Hicks. Braxton Hicks." I deadpanned.

"Cute."

"You'll get my real name when we're partners."

"You still haven't told me anything that proves you've got my data."

"All right. You snuck in using an unlisted phone number that you'd requested for Sally Boszik. On Fridays you waited until the buffer was loaded, then you degraded the data that was collected for the week. The significant drug effects would be invisible to Dr. Schatzkin's team. You kept the actual data elsewhere, on a subdirectory in Sally Boszik's name. Do you need more?"

Sylvia rotated her coffee cup while she calculated her options.

"So, what do you want?"

"I like that. Right to the bottom line. This is a business deal. First, a finder's fee. Say fifty thousand dollars cash. That's for the disk itself. Then I want to participate in the investment potential of what's on the disk. Say a percentage off the top of Palmetto Research. If you are onto something here, we all get rich together. If not, I've been paid for my time and considerable trouble and we go our separate ways."

"And if I say no?"

"I take this disk to the police and Dr. Schatzkin. I'm a good citizen and you're muff-diving for cigarettes in the Graybar Hotel. Trust me on this one. You're not cut out to do time. So, what'll it be?"

She sat there, her hands clasped to her mouth, a faraway look in her eyes. Inside she was running to every exit her mind could conjure and finding each one bricked up. Hope starts at a gallop. Then a prance. Then a trot. Outside the last door you're trudging uphill and there's no air to breathe.

"Okay, we'll do it your way," she said flatly.

"There you go. That wasn't so bad. Relax. This is going to work out just great. We're all going to be rich. You're going to be famous.

"Oh yeah, there's one more thing. The guy you hired to get this disk. He's going to have to be eliminated. That's my ticket of admission to this little gold mine."

"Why eliminated?"

"Because the guy you hired is a fucking psycho. He's already killed three people looking for this disk. He's like way over-extended, and I don't think that just saying no to him is going to cut it."

Sylvia's alarm at the death count seemed genuine, so I pressed on. "You didn't know any of this, did you?"

She shook her head.

"How did you think this guy was going to do your dirty work?"

"I don't know," she whispered.

I leaned over the table. "What did you tell him, then?"

She avoided my eyes and shrugged.

"So, yeah, he needs to be eliminated. He ties you to three

murders and he didn't get the disk. Jesus, I hope you're better in the lab than you are in the real world, Doc, or we're all fucked anyway."

"Don't worry about my competence in the lab. None of this would have happened if Schatzkin gave me the credit I was owed."

"Whatever. Just tell me about the guy."

She rested her head in her palm and dully recited the facts. "His name is Otto Kugler. Late twenties, no fixed address. Multiple drug abuser. PCP, grass, alcohol, you name it. Unemployed. I think he came out here from L.A. What else do you need to know?"

"How about a description?"

"About your size. Not so broad. Wiry. Very muscular, though. He's quite tanned. He's bald and he's got a van dyke beard. His face is deeply lined. He looks quite a bit older than he is."

"Anything else? What's the most distinctive thing about him?"

"I don't know. I didn't spend a whole lot of time with him, and I sure wasn't going to stare at him."

"Why not?"

"He was hyper to begin with, and real paranoid about our meeting."

"So, what do you remember most about him?"

"I don't know. His mouth, maybe."

"What about it?"

"He had no lips. Just this thin white line in his face. Like a scar that talked."

"All right. I'm going to take care of this guy. When it's done, I'll call you and we'll meet to conclude our business. You need to come up with fifty grand. So I'll let you get on it." I pushed away from the table and stood up.

"Uh, Mr. Hicks, this has all been quite entertaining, but inconclusive. On the offchance that you're a policeman, I don't think that I've admitted to anything other than having met a man named Otto Kugler. Of course, I've indulged your fantasies, but that was under duress, you breaking in here and holding me at gunpoint."

I shook my head. "Doctor, I have proof of everything I said to you. But I don't want to use it. You know, you being the goose with the golden egg and everything. Tell you what, though. I can see where you're coming from. You've got a lot more to fear from me than I do from you. That's no way for a relationship to begin. I think the answer is for us both to be dirty. I've got to kill Kugler anyway. How about I bring you his head for proof? Or any other part you want?"

She flinched, but didn't answer. I went on, "We've got a deal, Doc. I'm going to do my end. You do your end and we'll get along great. You don't, and this is all gone."

I walked over and fingered the lapel on her robe. "No more silk robes. No more fresh-brewed coffee. No croissants." I grabbed her chin. "Three months inside and you'll think Santa Claus brought you this deal."

As I walked out, I picked up my clipboard and left her knife on the table by the door.

Stepping through the doorway, I pulled it shut behind me. One down and one to go.

34

I climbed into Del's car. He had the phone in his hand.

"Cutting it close, aren't we?"

"Hey, that's big-time detective work, Del."

"Now what?"

"Sit on her. Make it an open shadow. If she knows she's being watched, I think she'll be good. She's got a lot to do. Don't get too close, though. I don't want her frightened, just aware." I slapped him on the thigh. "It's a time for subtlety, Del."

I got out of the car, and told him to call me on my beeper every three hours with a report on the surveillance.

Back at my own car, I stowed my gear in the trunk and began to think about my meeting with Otto Kugler. Exchanges are hell to arrange. Everybody wants the same protection, but they pose different threats to each other. I tried on scenarios from Kugler's point of view and then my own. I discarded lots of locations until I had one that worked for both of us.

A couple of phone calls completed my plans. There was nothing to do now but wait for Kugler to call.

Just after nine, my beeper went off. It was my office calling. I rang back and got Kelly.

"It's that guy, Leo. The one who called before. I told him you weren't here, but I could reach you. He's holding on line 22."

"Fine. Run it like a conference call. Call me on my car phone and I'll talk to him."

"Anything else?" she asked expectantly.

"No, Kelly. That's all."

"Okay," she said with some reluctance.

"Kelly, don't tape this one. Just hook up the calls and go downstairs for a donut. What you don't know won't hurt you."

"Okay."

I hung up and waited for her to ring me back. When she did, I let it ring twice. No need to look eager.

"Hello," I said.

"Time's up, Haggerty. You got the key?"

"I've got it. Let's just work out a way to make the exchange."

"I know a place. Down by the river. It's quiet. We won't get interrupted."

"No, thanks. A public place is more what I had in mind."

"Fuck that. How do I know it's not a trap? You could have cops all over the place."

"Right. And I'm going to some isolated spot with you. Guess again."

After a moment of silence, I started again.

"Look, I've got an idea. There's a pedestrian overpass on the Beltway. It's just north of the Braddock Road Exit. You approach it from the south and I will from the north. We pull our cars up under the overpass, get out and walk across to the other one's car, get in and drive away. I leave the key you want in my car. We make the exchange and everyone lives happily ever after."

"Wait a minute. Suppose there's no key in your car or it's the wrong key?"

"Then we're back to square one. I've got the key and you on my back. If I were going to stiff you, why bother with the exchange at all? I just tell you to fuck yourself and I disappear. No, I've had enough of this. I just want to get on with my life. You can have the key."

"Okay. Sounds good so far. An overpass is pretty exposed, though."

"Not this one. They had a jumper there, so now it's enclosed in a steel mesh. What are you worried about anyway, a sniper? Hell, bring a gun yourself. I don't care. When you get to your side of the overpass, start to cross with your arms up. I'll do the same. Either one of us goes for it, the other one can start blasting away. It's wide enough for us to pass each other without getting too close."

"Okay. Let's get it over, then."

"Wait a minute. What kind of car will you be driving?"

"A Jeep Cherokee. Dark blue."

"Okay, but I need a description, too. I don't even know what you look like."

"Yeah, right. Okay. I'm five feet ten, about 230. I'm wearing blue jeans and an orange T-shirt."

"Yeah, and . . ."

"And what?"

"So are you blond, bearded, wear glasses? I'm not getting out unless I know it's you on the other side."

"Yeah. I got blond hair. It's pulled back in a ponytail. No beard or nothing and I'll be wearing shades."

"Okay. I'm driving a steel gray BMW. Four doors. I'm about six feet tall . . ."

"Hey, don't bother, sport. I know what you look like. I saw enough pictures of you to last a lifetime."

"I'm sure you did. Let's get this over with. I can be at the overpass in ten minutes."

"Whoa. You picked the place. I'll pick the time. I'm nowhere near there. Say forty-five minutes."

"Fine. When I see you, I'll pull up to the overpass on my side. When we cut our engines, we get out together. Any delay on your part and I'm out of there. Got it?"

"Yeah, I got it."

"Hands overhead, just go straight to the overpass, and we walk across. The key will be on the front dashboard of the car. The ignition key will be in the lock. Just get in and drive away. When you're satisfied, call my office and leave a message where I can pick up the car. I'll leave one for you. And don't get any smart ideas. My car's a rental. I'll just have some stranger return it to the agency. This is where you get off."

"Yeah? You still gotta carry me for another forty-five minutes."

"I've got nine-thirty right now. What about you?"

"Yeah, nine-thirty."

"See you at ten-fifteen, then."

"That's a fact."

We hung up. Lying fuck. I twisted the key in the ignition, slapped the gears into first, and sped out of the lot.

Fifteen minutes later I got off the road and slowed to a halt. I could see the exchange point between the trees.

I pulled my Colt out of my holster and laid it on the seat next to me.

"Well, Arnie, how're we doing?" I said and looked into my rear-view mirror. His silence caught in my throat. I could almost see him there. The slick patches of skin on his face and head, the grafts that accepted no emotions, that conveyed no feelings. He'd say, "Enjoy it. Revenge is a luxury item. You've got to be able to keep score to even it. Most people can't count that high."

And what was our score? Twice he'd saved my life. Panczak's goons lay in unmarked graves in the Lorton woods. All three of them. Gutierrez's gunman in Georgetown. That was the score I wished I could even. This was too little and too late. "It's the best I can do, though," I said to no one in particular.

Too many times I'd consoled myself with the thought that Arnie would avenge me. That he was implacable and irresistible and on his way. How could I do less? He was a bastard, then an orphan. No wife, no children, some enemies, fewer friends, and no equals. If I would not do this for him, what he would do without a second thought, then he was never here at all.

That just left Sam. She was right. I'd played fast and loose with her. She'd asked me not to go out. My decision, but she'd paid the price. Everybody had paid a price except me and Otto. That wasn't fair. If you can't make something good, at least make it fair. It was time Otto and I paid our share. I closed my eyes, afraid that I might see how far short this fell. I pressed the Colt's barrel against my forehead and rubbed it back and forth. The metal was cold. And smooth. As smooth as the teardrops that would not fall.

35

Twenty minutes later the exchange began. I saw Kugler's Cherokee pull up. He got out of the car and he was armed. A sawed-off shotgun. Probably the one he killed Arnie with.

Just about time for me to pull up. And I would have, except the Jeep was now on the far side of the overpass and Kugler was crouched in the woods behind my side of the ramp. I wasn't at all surprised that a burly, clean-shaven blond climbed out of the Jeep and put his hands in the air.

It was okay though, because I was standing in the woods behind Kugler.

The gray BMW sedan pulled off the road and came down the shoulder. When it came to a halt, the driver put the key on the dashboard and turned off the motor.

Kugler waited until he heard the click of the door lock. He rushed out of his hiding place and fired a blast at the windows of the car. Hunched over with enthusiasm, he fired round after round into the car.

Inside, the driver turned and waved at Kugler. Masked by the noise of his firing, I charged through the woods until I stood just off his right shoulder.

Arms extended, all I saw was the notch in my sights. Startled, Kugler spun toward me, I centered the notch on his chest as his gun swung in a downward arc. He might have shot me. He might have thrown it down. I didn't wait to find out. I pulled the trigger and kept on pulling until the slide locked.

Kugler was on his back, arms out. He'd flung the shotgun behind him. I walked over to him. He had four holes in his chest, and a fifth where his left nostril used to be.

There was a screech of tires and I crouched and spun toward the road. The Cherokee was racing down the far shoulder. I straightened up and watched it disappear up the exit ramp.

Holstering my gun, I leaned over Kugler's body. "Now, you're off my back."

36

I walked over to the car. The door was sprayed with pellet holes and the window was a lattice of white fissures from the buckshot.

I pulled the door open and slid in. Davey Isaacs was smiling. He was an old friend and part of my groundwork for good luck. We had worked together as bodyguards, first for Franklin Security, then freelance.

"Go down like you figured?"

"Absolutely. He couldn't resist an ambush. I set it up so this one made the most sense. When he lied to me about his description, I knew he was going to do it."

"So you bushwacked the bushwacker."

"That's right." I shook my head. "Why'd you wave at him?"

"Distract him. Let him know he was fucked before it happened. So he'd go out knowing he'd been played for a chump."

"I hope so."

I turned and ran my fingers over the bulletproof glass in the window. Not a single pellet had penetrated. The Kevlar panels in the door had absorbed the rest of the buckshot.

"Thanks, Davey. I couldn't have done it without you."

"Hey, Leo. After you told me about Arnie and everything, how could I not help?"

"I couldn't assume it, though. It means a lot to me, Davey.
I won't forget it."

"Hey, I was glad to do it. You were cold, man, I'll tell you.
He was down, out, and gone, and you were still pulling the
trigger like he couldn't get dead enough to satisfy you."

"You're right about that. This'll have to do, though."

I reached down and picked up the car phone. Davey pulled
out a flask and offered me some as I dialed. I took a pull while
he was putting his housekey back on his ring, and gave it back
to him.

"Lieutenant Arbaugh, please. Tell him it's Leo Haggerty
calling. It's important."

"Haggerty, where are you?" he demanded when he got on
the line.

"Sitting in a car, Lieutenant. I called to tell you that I was
attacked today. I think it was the same man who attacked my
. . . uh . . . Samantha Clayton."

"Attacked you, huh? Are you okay?" he said without a hint
of concern.

"Yeah, I'm fine, Lieutenant."

"How about this guy? Can you describe him?"

"Oh, sure. Caucasian. About six feet, two hundred pounds,
bald. He's got a beard. Brown eyes."

"Any distinguishing marks?"

"Yeah. He's got them, too. Five bullet holes. A close group
in the chest and one in the nose . . ."

"Jesus Christ, Haggerty, where are you?"

"I'm on the shoulder of the Beltway. At the pedestrian overpass, right before the Braddock Road Exit."

"This guy, he's there, too?"

"Totally."

"Should we send an ambulance?"

"There's no rush."

"Shit, don't move. I'm on my way."

I hung up the phone and we waited. Ten minutes passed and
there was an ambulance, a cruiser with two uniformed officers,

the crime scene wagon, Arbaugh, and yellow tape going up everywhere. They impounded Davey's car and took my gun and Kugler's shotgun. They searched for the three slugs I fired into the trees, and issued an APB for the blue Jeep. Kugler was officially pronounced dead, tagged, bagged, and put into the ambulance. Davey and I got separate rides to the station house and separate audiences for our versions of what happened.

At the station I asked for my phone call and made it. Twenty minutes later Walter Reuther O'Neil knocked on the interrogation-room door.

Arbaugh looked over his shoulder, puckered his mouth in disgust, and waved him in. We'd been posturing for about ten minutes and I was bored. We'd done the iron-eyeball tango and the pigeon-chest puff-up. Then there was some assorted table banging and finger pointing by Arbaugh, which I countered with rolled eyes and wide-mouthed yawns.

"Lieutenant Arbaugh, I'm Walter O'Neil. I'd like to speak to my client alone, please."

"Yeah, sure. Make it snappy, though. We're ready to book him."

Walter smiled benignly, allowing Arbaugh his fiction of the inevitability of my fall.

He sat down and put his briefcase on the floor next to the table leg. Steepling his hands on the table, he nodded and said, "So, Leo, what have you done?"

I learned over the years how to read Walter. He had on the disinterested mask he wore when picking over the remains of someone else's folly. Poking into every corner of my tale to see whether, once again, he could in fact build a cathedral from a pile of bones. Had I been only a client, that was all I would have seen, at least at this time. But we were friends, and Walter registered the more damaging facts as if they had happened to him.

When I was finished, he bent down, pulled his case onto the table, popped it open, and took out a pad. He pulled a gold pen from his jacket pocket and began to make notes. He asked his questions, I gave my answers. Back and forth we went. He gave me his prognosis and his recommendations. I told him what I wanted. Eventually we had a workable plan. He leaned back and hooked his long pianist's fingers into his suspenders.

"Shall we?" The slightest smile lifted the corners of his mouth. The hawk had seen the rabbit.

I nodded in agreement. Walter stood up, buttoned his double-breasted jacket, pulled at his cuffs, and walked to the door.

He stuck his head outside and called for the lieutenant.

Arbaugh strode into the room. "Okay, Haggerty, you and your lawyer have had your little talk. Now it's our turn." He turned toward Walter and showed him the door with his thumb.

"Sorry, Lieutenant, I'm staying. You've got Mr. Isaacs's story. It's obviously a matter of self-defense. I want my client released."

"You want, you want," Arbaugh mimicked. "Climb this," he said, and waved a rigid digit. "No way am I letting this guy go. Murder One, and it'll stick."

"Are you kidding? You've got a car riddled with buckshot, fired from ambush. An eyewitness who says that Haggerty warned the man to drop his gun. The same witness says that he drew down on Haggerty. He shot to save his life. Self-defense pure and simple. You take this to the Commonwealth's attorney and she'll laugh you out of her office. Save yourself the grief, Arbaugh."

"Bullshit, O'Neil. Who're you trying to kid? You can spit-shine this turd all you want. I know what I'm looking at."

Arbaugh leaned forward and got right in my face. "You set this guy up, Haggerty. He murdered your friend and raped your woman. That's the motive. You knew what kind of guy he was. So you let him think he had the drop on you. Your buddy sitting in his bulletproof car wasn't in any danger. You waited until his gun was empty. Then you jump out and blow him away. Murder One. Not self-defense. I got motive, opportunity, and means. You killed this guy just like he killed your friend. No difference, Haggerty. Those are the facts and facts don't change."

"Lieutenant, you have your facts and I have mine. I'm quite confident that the Commonwealth's attorney and a jury will prefer my facts. In fact, why don't we ask her to come down here and see what she has to say? Save everybody a lot of trouble."

Arbaugh wheeled toward Walter. Thank God they were both experienced, and had been cured of their idealism. Silently, they probed each other's will, looking for the slightest doubt or hesitancy, then checking their own resolve. No one wants to take a loser into court. There're too many battles waiting to be fought, and each loss takes something out of you. Something you can't put back.

"Okay, I'll call. We'll see what she says. Until then, O'Neil, you're out of here. Now move."

"Of course, Lieutenant, whatever you say." Walter picked up his briefcase, nodded to me, and went out into the hall. Arbaugh looked at me with disdain and walked out. I sat at the burned and scarred metal table and stared at the gray cinder-block walls. I would never know what turned it in Arbaugh's mind. Maybe that Kugler wasn't such a prince and he couldn't get worked up over scumbags shooting scumbags. Let us thin our own herd. Then nuke the ones that are left.

I did my first hour sitting at the table. Every once in a while, one of the cops put his face in the window. I checked to see how I felt about killing Kugler. Nothing. Maybe Sam had been wrong. Maybe I'd already changed and we didn't know it. I was attentive to that possibility but not alarmed, like finding a benign tumor.

Besides, Kugler had his chance. I really didn't know what I was going to do until I got there. Even while his gun was swinging toward me. Warn him? Shoot him? Maybe nothing at all. Somewhere in there I made my decision.

By the end of the second hour, I was alternating between sitting on the table and circling it. The door opened and Walter strode in, slim and elegant in his pinstripe suit. Behind him strode the Commonwealth's attorney, also slim and elegant in her pinstripe suit.

They slammed their briefcases on the table, looked at me for a second, and went back to their conversation.

"I won't do it, Walter. He's not going to walk on this one. Not like this. I need something in return. I've talked to Rhodasson and Arbaugh. They were looking for Kugler, too. They know that he killed Kendall and raped Samantha Clayton. They even know why."

"And that is?" he asked casually.

"Because he thought they had a key that had been stolen from him by Harold Snipes. That's what this is all about. I want that key and everything that goes with it. For starters."

"Who's this Snipes?" he asked.

"Another scumbag," she said, dismissing him with a wave of her hand. She turned to me. "We're not morons, Haggerty. We put the two of you together bringing in Snipes. He was already going into the Witness Protection Program. He rolled over on you for seconds at lunch. So we know all about the key. Let's start there."

Walter smiled at her. His requiem grin. "And you know me, Lisa," he said, shaking his head.

"Yeah, 'No-deal O'Neil.' Well then, counselor, I'll see you in court, when we go to set bail." She nodded her head and made to leave.

"Whoa, let's not get carried away here," I said and approached the Commonwealth's attorney.

Walter introduced us. "Leo Haggerty, my client. Leo, your jailer, Commonwealth's attorney, Lisa Monroe."

"Let me get this straight. If I give you the key or what it was to, you'll drop the charges?"

Lisa looked at Walter before she said anything.

"If I don't like what's going on, I'll jump in," Walter said, not smiling now.

"I didn't say that. I said you absolutely weren't walking without my getting something in return." She motioned for me to sit and stood back with her arms crossed. Lisa Monroe was a tangle of copper hair, hazel eyes, and pale freckled skin. Round-rimmed glasses added to her serious demeanor.

"Suppose I can help you clear up a bunch of crimes. All felonies. Front page of the *Post* stuff."

"I'm listening."

"Uh, excuse me. If we're going to do this, I think we ought to agree to some terms up front." Walter was in.

"Such as?"

"Absolute immunity for my client from all charges in this matter. In return he gives you whatever he has."

"No. He tells me what he has first, then I decide if it's a deal."

"No way, Lisa. Immunity first, then he talks."

"Uh, can I get in here, boys and girls?"

"Yes, Mr. Haggerty?"

"How about I give you this." I raised a hand to ward off Walter's blazing stare. "I can solve two other murders for you. In addition, I can give you the people who hired Kugler and the whole conspiracy he was part of. You know he wasn't the whole thing. If you haven't pulled his rap sheet, you'll find out soon enough. He was a loser. A druggie, a psycho. The guy thought Elvis was hiding out with Hitler. Without me you'll never get to the people behind him. I can connect them. Nobody else can. He can't roll over on anyone. He killed everyone else who knew about him. I walk on this and in return I give you the whole package. That's my deal, whether my attorney agrees or not."

Monroe liked it. She liked the idea of getting the first deal ever off of "No-deal O'Neil," even if it was over his objection and noted with an asterisk. She liked what I was offering, too.

"All right. It's a deal. Absolute immunity from all charges in today's shooting in exchange for complete cooperation, including testifying, in regards to two murders by Kugler, and in indicting and trying the persons who hired him, for all crimes arising from and pertaining to their conspiracy with Otto Kugler."

I checked with Walter. He nodded gravely.

"It's a deal."

37

I called Sylvia Francis from the Commonwealth attorney's office. Lisa Monroe was downstairs presenting a motion to one of the circuit court judges.

"Hello," Sylvia said.

"Hello, there, partner. Remember me? I think it's time we got together to discuss our mutual interests."

"I can't. I don't have the money. It's too soon."

"Hell, don't worry about the money. I know you're good for it. I think we should meet just to get acquainted. Sort of like a first date, you know. We're gonna be in this together for a long time. We have some serious shit on each other. You know. Show some good faith."

"All right, all right, what do you want?"

"How about dinner? A nice public place. We'll all be on our best behavior. Talk about your plans, my plans. Where we're going together. How about Artie's? Early, before it's crowded, so we can talk without being overheard."

"Whatever. When do you want to meet?"

"How about six?"

"Fine. What about the matter we discussed this morning?"

"You mean Kugler? Don't worry. I'll bring proof with me. He's past tense. Tell you what, though. Check out the five o'clock news. I'll bet they run something on it. Beltway shoot-outs don't happen every day."

"Anything else?"

"Just one thing. Bring along your partner, Fanny Shoate. It's her company I'm saving. I think we should meet."

Nothing. "You there? Did you hear me?"

"Yeah. I heard you." The words leaked out of her like the air in an old tire.

"Six, then," I said, and hung up.

Lisa Monroe strode into the room and told me to get the hell out of her chair. Walter smiled and Arbaugh shook his head.

"All right. Everything has been approved. Did you set up a meeting?"

I nodded.

"Great. Go on downstairs with Lieutenant Arbaugh. He'll get everything ready. I'll meet you there in ten minutes."

She dismissed us by scribbling some notes on a pad. We rose in unison and moved toward the door. She looked up.

"Walter, that promise of immunity you got depends on your client's performance. Remind him of that. If he doesn't tie these women to Kugler, tight, I'll settle for him."

"Lisa, he's doing you a favor. If he doesn't deliver them to you with an apple in their mouths, you'll have nothing. I'll walk him on this, believe it."

"If he does his job, we won't have to find out, will we?"

"See you downstairs, Lisa."

Walter and I walked down the hall, letting Arbaugh lead.

"Did you hear all that?" he asked.

"Yeah. Let her talk. I don't really care."

"You should, Leo. She's a good attorney. I've seen stigmata appear on witnesses after she's cross-examined them."

"Don't worry, Walter. I have every intention of tying these two to Kugler. Like a cement block around their ankles. Then I'm gonna push them in, and it's gonna be perfectly legal. We're all going to get what we want."

"Hurry up, you two, I don't have all day," Arbaugh barked from the elevator.

At six o'clock I walked into Artie's. I told the hostess I wanted an upper booth in the back and followed her down the aisle. I settled in, and put my envelope on the table. A waitress came by and asked if I wanted a drink. I said no and admired what she did for a long-sleeved white shirt, black slacks, bow tie, and suspenders.

I watched the front door from my seat. At ten after, they walked in. Sylvia scanned the room and I waved her back. She led the way and Shoate trudged along behind. It was the woman from the pavilion at Nottaway Park. They slid in opposite me and released anxious smiles, as if good manners were a vaccine for bad news.

"Hello, ladies," I said, and stuck out my hand. Sylvia passed; Fanny, docile Fanny, shook it briefly.

"Excellent. Glad you could both make it. I think we're going to be together a long time and do some great things. What do you say we start with some wine?"

"Why don't we skip the pleasantries, Mr. . . . ?" Sylvia said curtly.

"Haggerty. And you are Sylvia Francis and Fanny Shoate. Fine, let's skip the pleasantries and get right down to business."

The waitress returned and took my order for an Irish whiskey neat, Sylvia's Perrier with a twist, and Fanny's Coke.

"You know, Sylvia, I've been doing some thinking since we met this morning and you've got me worried. Men don't seem to fare too well around you. First, you sabotage Schatzkin's research project because you were annoyed at how he treated you. Then you hire Kugler to kill Onslow because he wouldn't do what you wanted. Then you let me waltz in and remove Kugler because he was a liability. I think there's a pattern here. But that's okay, because I have a solution for it. Trust. That's what we need. I don't want to spend my time worrying about whether you're out there lining somebody up to replace me.

The answer is . . ." Our drinks arrived and I stopped to sip mine.

". . . How to make what's good for you good for me, too. You're real good at looking out for yourself. So I figure if that's good for me too, then I can turn my back on you now and then. Okay? How do we do this? I think we have to get down and dirty together. Equally, so that there's no percentage in betraying each other or replacing each other. And out of that dungheap the beautiful flowers of mutual trust will grow."

I sipped my drink and eyed them both. Sylvia was a blank. Fanny had a little tic in her left eye.

I slipped two mini-recorders out of my pocket and put them on the table next to the envelope.

"Okay, you're over there, saying to yourselves, How do I know this guy is for real? How do I know he has the data? How do I know he isn't a cop? This is how."

I pushed one recorder over to Sylvia. She looked at it like it was a chocolate-covered roach.

"Pick it up. It won't bite you. Now, to answer the first question, I'm going to show you that I killed Otto Kugler. That puts me in a heap of shit. But that's okay, because you're going to tell me how and why you hired him, and that puts you in a heap of shit, because old Otto, he killed three people and raped another one while he was working for you, so that's like you did it yourselves. That puts us equally in the shit and it's as good a basis for a partnership as I can think of." I took another sip and wondered who was saying these words.

"See, I'm going to give you a confession of my part and then you're going to do the same thing for me."

Fanny's head had been slowly slumping forward. All I could see now was the top. I tapped her wiry hair. "Hey, buck up, Fanny. We're almost done. You get your company sold, you get to be rich. We all get to be rich. Hang in there.

"I'm going to tell you what happened to old Otto, and while I do, I'm going to tape it all on this little recorder. See, here's the tape. The battery light is on. It works just fine. When I'm done, I'm going to hold on to this. Then you're going to do the same thing and tell me all about how you hired Otto and so on. Then we'll exchange recorders. We'll both have each other's confessions. I'd recommend giving it to your lawyer to turn over to the police if anything bad happens to either one of you. That's what I'm going to do."

They sat there, silent, impassive. Shoate, I guessed, felt like she was being measured for a casket. The deeper the barrel she was in, the greater her torpor. Wait till she finds out that this one has no bottom. Francis was taking it all in, but I knew she was scheming all the time. Working all her options. Trying out how to counter my pressure. Above all, it was her voice I wanted on that tape.

"For starters, let me convince you of my sincerity." I opened the envelope and slid out three Polaroids of Otto Kugler. The first was a shot of his body on the ground, in the awkward sprawl of sudden death, his arms outflung like he'd thrown his life away.

Nothing from Sylvia. Fanny shuddered and looked away.

Number two was a close-up of Kugler's face. Head on. Eyes closed, he looked like he was sleeping. Kugler wasn't such a bad-looking guy. Strong, even features. Except for that third nostril leaking down his cheek.

Sylvia was still going strong. Shoate looked like a salted snail. I pushed on.

The last one was Kugler's chest. His shirt was off and the four holes made an italic *N* between his nipples. He was well muscled, deeply tanned, and served in a pool of his own blood.

"All right, enough," Sylvia snapped.

"Hey, I just wanted you to be sure. This is serious business and I'm a serious guy." I picked up my recorder and clicked it on. "This is Leo Haggerty speaking. The date is November 12, 1990, and I'm speaking without coercion or duress. On this date I shot Otto Kugler five times, causing his death. This act took

place at approximately ten-thirty a.m. in the wooded area behind the pedestrian overpass near the Braddock Road Exit of
the outer loop of the Beltway."

I clicked off my tape and nodded at the two of them. Shoate
winced and grabbed Sylvia's arm.

"Do we have to?"

"Yes, damn it. He has the data I need."

Sylvia thumbed down the recorder and began: "My name is
Sylvia Francis. The date is November 12, 1990, and I am speaking without coercion or duress." She stopped.

"What do you want?"

"How about starting with Terry Onslow. You can turn that
thing off. This is just for my curiosity. I want to know if I got
this right."

The waitress returned and asked if we were ready to order.
We took refills on our drinks and I added some fried calamari
to sop up some of the excess whiskey in me.

"Terry Onslow found out that I was getting into the system
and what I was doing. He sent me a message by electronic mail,
asking me what I was doing. I told him I was running an al-
ternative statistical analysis. He knew I wasn't because it wasn't
indexed for the other investigators. So when I couldn't bluff
him, I tried to bribe him. We met. I told him I was working
for another company now. He told me that he'd think about
it. I decided to get out of the system and leave them with the
false data. When I went back for it, it was gone. He'd hidden
my data. So I said let's meet my boss. He said no. He wasn't
interested. He was going to tell Schatzkin about what I'd done.
I couldn't let him do that. I'd worked too hard to come up with
nothing."

"That's not the way I heard it. Schatzkin said you weren't
pulling your weight. You wanted your own projects but your
ideas didn't merit the resources."

"That's a lie. Schatzkin's an egomaniac. He thinks he's the
only one that has an idea worth pursuing. Nobody else. Especially a woman. We're only good for getting coffee for the

big boys. There was no way I was going to be forced out and start over from scratch, like some graduate school lab assistant. Those compounds were my work, too. They could force me out, but not empty-handed. I made sure that I could get the benefits of that data, and all the work I did."

"Why not sneak in, duplicate the data, and take it out of the system?"

"Because my PC wouldn't run the package I needed to analyze the data. Anyway, I had to keep going back to look at each week's data. I needed them to augment my trials and accelerate my results. They keep moving up the criteria for effectiveness. You don't want to miss anything. It used to be that you had to wait for full infection to set in, but that takes years. Now they're looking for highly correlated chemical changes that will tell you whether AIDS will take hold or not. The damned activists keep changing the rules, trying to hurry everything up."

"And with everything that's at stake, too. All that money. Careers. Reputations."

"What's that supposed to mean?" she snapped.

"Nothing. Just pumping a little irony. It's how I stay in shape."

"You should be careful. It might fall on you."

"That's touching. I think we're getting to the good part. Why don't you tell the recorder about Otto Kugler."

She thumbed the recorder again and began. "I located Otto Kugler at some skinhead bar. I knew about him and his run-in with Dr. Schatzkin from a previous research study. He wanted to be part of a study on analgesics and chronic head pain. Dr. Schatzkin rejected him because his psychological profile showed him to be likely to abuse the medications instead of following the prescriptions. I offered him a chance to get back at Schatzkin and make some money, too."

"You sure that was all? You sure you didn't tell him about the research he was 'derailing'? All those poor dumb pregnant nigger bitches." I flashed a look at Shoate. "I mean, that's the

biggest population you were studying, right? Most of the pregnant women with AIDS are junkies and hookers, right? And
most of them are black or Hispanic, right? You don't look well,
Fanny. Did you miss out on this part before?"

"No, Mr. Haggerty, that's not how it was. Whatever story
Mr. Kugler concocted to boast to his friends was his creation.
My offer was strictly money."

I pointed to the recorder.

"I offered Mr. Kugler ten thousand dollars to get my data
back from Terry Onslow."

I shook my head. "Well, you got what you paid for. So Kugler
says to you, 'What if he doesn't want to give it to me? What
should I do?' "

Sylvia's voice grew quiet and curiously flat, without inflection
or timbre. "I told him I didn't care. Do what you have to. I
just don't want to know about it." She clicked off the recorder.

"Thank you, Dr. Francis. I think that puts you in the stall
next to me. Your turn, Ms. Shoate. You're head of an 8A
company, near the end of your run. You're not competitive.
No more easy money. No government handouts. Along comes
Dr. Francis. She tells you what a whiz-bang she is. She's got
the hot new AIDS drug she's working on. So you hitch yourself
to this rising star. You'll sell your company to one of the biggies.
Take the millions or so they pay you. Retire rich and young.
Out of the rat race. A credit to your race and gender. Now you
just jump right in here."

"Honest, I didn't know what the money was for originally.
She said it was for more equipment. But I never got any receipts
so I went to her and asked for an explanation. She said there
was a problem. That the guy at BMR who was helping her
transfer her data from there was trying to blackmail her. It was
the first I knew that she was using their data for her trials, I
swear . . ."

"So you told her to stop, right?" The squid arrived and I
squeezed some lemon over them.

"No. I gave her the money. She told me we were very close

to a major breakthrough. I had a buyer lined up for the company. If we had the data to support our claims, they were willing to buy us out completely."

"So what was the price? Ten percent of that is mine. Off the top."

Fanny looked at Sylvia for guidance and found none. "Three point two million."

"How much was deferred?"

"None. Cash at time of sale."

"Three hundred twenty thousand. Plus my finder's fee. Oh, this is sweet."

"I didn't know anything about this man Kugler, or anybody being killed. I swear it. I thought it was blackmail, that's all."

"That might have been true for a while, Fanny. But you're here now. And I saw Sylvia here give you the bad news. Just a couple of days ago in Nottaway Park. Am I right?"

"Yes. Yes. She told me that the blackmail money hadn't worked. That somebody else had the data and what you wanted. I told her I didn't have that kind of money. The company's on the verge of bankruptcy. All our contracts are ending and we haven't won a single one on our own."

"Bummeroo."

She went on. "I told her this had to stop. We couldn't go any further. That's when she told me everything. About hiring that man Kugler, and what you said. And the rest of it."

"Let's go, Fanny. Confession's good for the soul. Speak right into the mike."

She fumbled with the recorder. Sylvia took it from her, turned it on, and handed it back to her.

After her preamble, she admitted, "Sylvia Francis told me that a man, who I now know is Leo Haggerty, said he would kill Otto Kugler, and provide us with the data necessary to complete her research and sell our company. I agreed to pay Mr. Haggerty for his services by giving him a percentage off the top from the sales of my company, Palmetto Research Corporation."

She clicked off the recorder and laid it on the table.

"Is that sufficient?"

"Yeah. It'll do nicely. Looks like we've got a deal here. I'm not happy about giving up that front money, but I'll just tack it onto my money off the top."

"What about the data?" Sylvia asked.

"No problem, partner. First, let's exchange recorders."

I set mine out in the middle of the table, pulled my hand away in renunciation, and waited for them to reciprocate.

They looked at my tape, then my face, then their tape, then back to me again, like reluctant brides wondering what they were doing at the altar.

" 'Til death do us part, ladies. There's three point two million reasons to go forward. That's quite a pot of gold. What'll it be?"

Shoate's meager will was sapped. She began her slump of surrender. Francis slid their recorder next to mine.

"Tomorrow, after I've deposited this, I'll come by your offices and deliver your data and the disk. You can draw up the note for my money and I'll take that in return."

I leaned forward and chased the last bits of squid around the plate. Finishing them, I said, "How about drinks to celebrate? Champagne? My treat."

Sylvia said nothing. All that had gone before was one long involved insult, and it was just dawning on her that she would have to take it.

"No, thanks. I don't feel much like celebrating," Fanny said wearily.

"Really, why not? Is it the death count? Don't let that bother you. Next, you'll start thinking about all those pregnant girls, dying already, praying to God for something that'll spare their babies from paying for their mistakes. All the ones still getting sugar pills because no one knows that the other drug works. Christ, you start thinking about that, next it'll be all the babies that are gonna die. It just goes on and on."

They didn't answer. Both of them were staring over my shoulder at the mirrored back wall. Arbaugh and two policemen stormed up the aisle toward us.

Arbaugh's mouth was set in a tight, grim line. Knowing how he savored his rectitude, he must have been quite a happy man.

Sylvia grabbed the tape off the table before I could get it. She spun sideways in the booth and pulled a lighter from her purse. Popping out the tape, she held it to the lighter. First, it melted, then the cassette caught fire. Finally she dropped it on the table. As I poured water on the molten plastic, she snarled her vindication at me. "You've got nothing. Nothing. Do you hear me?"

Fanny was starting to hyperventilate. She shook her head from side to side and tried to say "No," but her gaping mouth hung empty. She couldn't hold enough air to make the sound.

I shook my head in commiseration. "Looks like there's no pot of gold after all. We must be sitting at the wrong end of the rainbow."

Sylvia would not go quietly. She could hardly wait for her rights to be read when she grabbed Arbaugh's lapels and tried to turn him toward me.

"What about him? This man's a murderer!" Arbaugh handed her to one of the officers. He reached over and guided Fanny out. She was still silently shaking her head. Arbaugh refused to look at me. The one that got away.

Sylvia leaned back against the policeman guiding her out, and screamed at me: "That man's a murderer! A murderer!"

I shook my head sadly as if they were the ravings of a mad-woman. Still, no one approached my table.

38

Commonwealth Attorney Monroe and Walter O'Neil slid into the booth. I detached the button microphone from my collar and handed it to her. I put the recorder in my pocket. She didn't need it.

"That was pretty slick, Mr. Haggerty."

I shrugged. "Stage magic, that's all. I didn't want them worried about whether I was wired and searching me. So I stuck the recorders right under their noses and petted them and made like they were our best friends."

"Well, it worked. We've got plenty on both of them, and it's all good stuff. The chain of evidence is sound. No question of alteration of the tapes. Plenty of witnesses to what they said. It'll be a pleasure putting them away." She shook her head. "Greedy pigs. What they did to those girls and their babies."

"I don't know. I don't think it was greed. They just felt entitled to it. Somebody owed it to them. They were just making sure things were fair. You can do anything thinking like that."

"Not in Fairfax County, Mr. Haggerty." She wasn't smiling. "By the way, we informed D.C. about that girl you said you found, and Terry Onslow turned up in the morgue. He'd been there as a John Doe for three days. Some campers found the body down in Mason Neck. He was pretty messed up. Some animals had been at him, but the burned palms were a match. Well, I have to leave. I'll see you tomorrow, Mr. Haggerty. Bring the data disk and any other evidence you have. We'll take your statement, too. When you testify, you're out of the woods."

"He'll be there, Lisa. He's done everything he said he would."

"See you tomorrow, Walter," she said, and left.

"What now, Leo?"

"I don't know. I guess I'll go home. See if Sam's there. See if I can get out of her woods."

"Is there anything I can do?"

"No, but thanks for asking."

"If there is, just call. And I'm sorry about Arnie and Sam."

"I know."

We said goodbye outside the restaurant. I watched him walk to his car, get in, and pull away. Such a simple action. I couldn't get myself to move or to go anywhere. I'd finished my agenda, done what I wanted to do. And for my efforts I had a fistful of empty. Now I had to honor the claims others had on me, and I couldn't move.

I don't know how long I stood there. There really was nowhere to go. I was a man on fire. If I ran from myself, I'd only fan the flames. I stood there until I surrendered to that fact. Once I had surrendered, I was free to leave and go where I had to.

39

The office was closed, but I entered carefully. I didn't want to see anyone, and hoped that no one was being ambitious.

I walked by Kelly's desk and peered down the hall. The office doors were open. Each room was dark and silent. I sat on her desk, called my answering service, and left a message for Schafrath Brown to bring Randi home. Grateful for my employee's punctuality, I opened the door to my office. The urn was not on my desk. If that asshole . . . No, there it was on the file cabinet. I picked it up. It was obscenely light, a lie to the weight of my memories. We were so far apart that even in my hands, I couldn't recognize my friend. Cremation is an atheist's act of faith. Everything is here, left behind, and never to be seen again.

"Let's go home, Arnie," I said, carrying my friend out of one darkness to another.

His house was a ruin, like mine. I placed the urn on a table, stepped past the overturned furniture, and walked down the hall to his armory. Arnie had no will and no family. The courts would appoint an executor to pay his taxes and debts and to dispose of his property. The money from that sale would go to the state. I know. I tracked down a number of lost heirs to stop just that from happening. I was only a friend and had no rights to anything of his. That was okay. I had no intention of arguing about it.

I pushed open the door to the armory. There was plenty of damage inside. Kugler hadn't been able to open Arnie's gun cases, so he'd pushed them over and defaced them with whatever was handy. Many of the other weapons he couldn't use, so he trashed them. The blowguns, crossbows, and calthrops were strewn all over the place.

I cared about one thing. Arnie's sword. Kugler had thrown it into a corner. Philistine that he was, he had no idea that it was the most valuable thing in the house. Four years in the making. The work of Japan's last living swordmaker of national treasure rank. All of that was nothing to me either.

The samurai's soul is his sword. His life is the tempering of his will until it is as pure and decisive as the edge of his blade. Then they are one. I reached down and picked up the sword. It was undamaged. I found the lacquered wooden sheath and slid the blade inside.

I took the blade with me back to the foyer. There I picked up Arnie's ashes, and made my way across his living room and out the patio door to his garden.

I knelt before the pool on the stone where Arnie used to meditate. Bonsai and white stone slabs were terraced around the waterfall that filled the pool. I placed the blade beside me and held the urn in my hands.

Goodbye, Arnie. Not many have the courage to live the way you did. Certainly not I. You were a mighty foe and a loyal friend. I'll miss your cockeyed sense of humor that relished every adversity. Like your blade, your honor shone in every light. I hope you knew that.

He who saves a life is responsible for it. That's what they say. Twice you took that burden. I hope it wasn't too heavy. You are only memories now, but they are good ones. Very good ones. You will be missed.

I stared into the pool until I had composed my death poem. I opened the lid of the urn and slowly shook the ashes into the pool. They drifted downward, dissolving and then disappearing. I spoke as the last ones fell on the water.

The stone mountain sleeps.
The last storm has passed his slopes.
Somewhere it is spring.

40

Before I left Arnie's house, I called Sam and told her that it was safe to go home and that I was on my way there.

I pulled up facing the house and cut the engine. It looked like my house, a place where I was welcome. The familiarity was deceptive. The shape was the same. The basic matter unchanged, but something ineffable was altered. Each surface, each item had been seasoned with memories. Like me, they had vibrated to the harmony of laughter and been battered by harsh words, absorbed tears one day and the sweat of delight on others. Tonight, that was missing. All the history had been buffed away.

I walked past Sam's car, and noted that it was parked on the street. What did that mean? Home, but reluctantly? Not quite here? Ready to go?

There was a light on in the living room, but the rest of the house was dark. I pulled open the storm door and walked into my future.

Everything was right where I left it. On the floor. Sam sat in the slashed recliner. The pole lamp next to it was on and shone down on her. She was wearing a long black leather coat. Her hands were stuffed deep in the pockets, like she was afraid of what they might do with room to move.

"Hello, Sam," I said, unwilling to presume a response from her, either affection or anger.

"Hello, Leo. Are you okay?" Her voice denied the question its weight.

"I'm okay," I lied.

We stood there, two strangers in familiar bodies. I'd been the first one to break the spell of trust. Now I was someone she didn't really know. A stranger who had brought terror, then pain, then sorrow inside these walls. Inside of her.

I looked at her face but couldn't really see her. I saw the stranger there. I knew the chestnut mane, the emerald eyes, the generous mouth, but they told me nothing. Once I could read the dilation of the eye, the turn of the head. The countless signs of animation and their meaning. Now it was a death mask. I had been revealed as the man she did not know. Every fact was now fiction. Every memory a dream. Our history now a myth.

Once, we had made a path that could not lead to this place. She could either deny her bruises, her empty womb, or who she thought I was. They could not both be true.

I had no idea what she would do, how she would choose. I knew what I wanted, what I hoped for.

I looked at Sam but did not see her because I was afraid of what I would find there. I refused to read anything into her face and called her inscrutable.

I stood there, in silence, afraid that anything I might say would come out as a plea for clemency that I knew I did not deserve. I took Sam's silence as rejection. Maybe it wasn't and I just needed it to be.

Eventually, I found my tongue and spoke. "Sam, I'm sorry about everything . . ."

She pulled her hand from her coat and held it up to stop me.

"Don't, Leo. Don't say anything. I've thought a long time about what I'm going to say and I don't have the strength to discuss it or defend it. Don't make this any harder on me than it already is, please."

If she'd asked, I'd have shot myself right there.

She stood up, with both her hands hidden again, and rushed through the words, not sure she had the will to declare what she knew she felt.

"Leo, I know you didn't mean for any of this to happen. But it did, and it did because you were careless with us. I asked you to come home and be with me, Leo, but you didn't. You felt you owed it to Arnie to be with him. You made the choice. Everything else flows from that, Leo. What happened to me, the baby, everything. You made the decision but I paid for it. He raped me, not you. I know you feel bad, but it's not the same. And I know you've lost a lot, too. Believe me, I'm not doing this to punish you, but every time I look at you, it all comes back to me. I blame you and I can't talk myself out of it, and I've tried. I'm so angry right now, I just don't want to be around you. And I don't trust you anymore.

"Leo, I used to look at you and only feel how lucky I was. That's been destroyed. I look at you and all I can feel is how much I've lost. I know you love me, Leo, but I don't think it's a love I can use. I can't rely on it. I think you'd give me everything you have, but I don't think it's what I need. I need to be first, Leo. I need someplace where I can count on that being true. That I won't be ignored or passed over for something or someone else. I know you tried. I know that's why you took this job. I just don't know that you can really do it, and I can't stand not knowing that.

"We paid a hell of a price for that one wrong decision. I don't think I can go through it again. I need to be away from you, Leo. Maybe that'll change. I don't know. But it's how I feel right now. I'll come back for my stuff later. When you're at work. Please don't come home. I'd rather not do it with you around. Okay?"

I nodded.

"Please don't call me, Leo. If I change my mind, I'll call you. I need to be alone to sort this out. Okay?"

"Sure. Anything you want."

"I'm going to go now. Goodbye, Leo."

She hurried toward me and I turned to let her pass. She kept her face away from me as she went by. I almost reached out to touch her shoulder, not to stop her, just to touch her as she left, but I didn't. I stood there and watched her walk away into the ripening darkness.

Night drew its lid down over the earth and the last faint light of day fled into the past. With it went my heart and the first tears began to fall.